A Desperate Frame-up

In This Series

That First Heady Burn
True Vermilion
The Dark Shill
A Stack of Sawbucks
The Hillside Roble
The Peroxide Pomp
The Incidental Twin
Brawl in Bardo
The Window-Shade Job
The Convenient Patsy
The Artisanal Grifter
Shrink in the Shadows
Project Chartreuse
From a Desert Playa
The Tired Canary
A Desperate Frame-up
Trail of the Blue Agave
The Saucer-Heads

A Desperate Frame-up

A Desperate Frame-up

George Bixley

DAGMAR
MIURA
LOS ANGELES

Published by Dagmar Miura
Los Angeles
www.dagmarmiura.com

A Desperate Frame-up

First published 2022

ISBN: 978-1-956744-58-3

ONE

H IS NECKTIE FELT LIKE it was choking him, and Slater pulled at his collar to loosen it. Perched on the witness stand with a microphone in his face, he tried to focus on the defense attorney's questions. It was a stupid insurance fraud case that he'd only worked on tangentially, and he had no interest in it, unsure what the nebbishy guy at the defense table was even charged with. But you can't ignore a subpoena.

"Mr. Ibáñez," the defense attorney said, "can you tell us who in the district attorney's office interviewed you regarding this case?"

Slater kind of liked this guy. He was the no-bull-shit type, and had the same dark Latin coloring as Slater. Despite his rumpled suit and bad haircut, he was basically fuckable.

"I didn't retain their names," Slater said, "but they're both sitting right there."

"Can you point them out for the court?"

Slater gestured vaguely to the table where the prosecutors sat. "The lowlife one, and the bougie one."

"Who is it that you characterize as a lowlife?"

"The bottle blond with the cheap blue suit," Slater said.

The blond rose, a scowl on his face. "Objection, your honor. At the very least I'm owed the respect of not being called cheap."

The defense attorney spoke louder. "Your honor, for the record, the witness characterized the honorable assistant district attorney as a lowlife, and said his suit was cheap."

"Enough, both of you," the judge said. She hadn't spoken much today, but right now she looked pissed. "Mr. Ibáñez, you will confine yourself to direct answers. Leave the judgment calls to me."

The defense attorney met his gaze. "And the individual you characterize as bougie?"

"The one with the bougie gray suit," Slater said, gesturing to her, "and the bougie Westside haircut, and the bougie pumps with the red soles. I don't wear heels, but I know those are expensive."

The woman glared at him, murder in her eyes. Slater could see that both of the prosecutors were fuming. A minute later, when it was his turn, the blond rose and met his gaze.

"Mr. Ibáñez, you characterized my suit as cheap. Do you work in the fashion industry? Are you perhaps a sartorial specialist? How much do you think this garment cost?"

The defense attorney quickly stood up. "Objection. Relevance."

"Sustained," the judge said. "Counselor, you need

to grow thicker skin."

"A different question, then," the blond said. "Mr. Ibáñez, why do you harbor animosity toward me personally?"

"I actually don't," Slater said. "I don't remember your name, and honestly, I don't care whether you live or die."

It went on like that, the guy blowing hot air, trying to squelch the defense attorney's implication that the prosecutors had threatened Slater, or promised him something. It wasn't true—Slater had done a straightforward debrief with them. But the defense guy just asking the questions in open court was effective. It made the prosecutors look calculating and manipulative.

After all the posturing, Slater actually answered a few substantive questions about the man who was on trial, and what he'd seen, and then it was over, he was dismissed, and the court recessed for the day.

In the hallway outside the courtroom, Slater headed toward the exit, but the defense attorney stepped up, a broad smile on his face.

"You make an excellent witness," he said.

"I thought some of what I said would be bad news for your client."

"Inevitably it was. But you come off as credible."

"I suppose it's because I don't really care about your client," Slater said, resting his hands on his hips, "or about you, or the prosecutors. I have so few fucks left to give, I have to ration them."

The guy raised his eyebrows. "That's what makes you credible. Listen, have you ever done any process serving?"

"No way, brother." Slater shook his head. "That's small-time stuff. Save it for your unpaid interns."

The blond prosecutor stepped up to them, his lip curling into a sneer. "You backstabbing little fuck."

"What, you wanted me to lie for you?" Slater said.

"Trash-talking my suit." He looked him up and down. "As if you're a snappy dresser—an ill-fitting thrift-store shirt and a clip-on tie. You look like every *cholo* I've ever prosecuted."

Slater leaned toward him and slapped him hard across the face, left and then right, a rapid kovac.

The guy flinched, and his eyes grew wide as he touched his cheek with his palm. "Are you fucking kidding me?"

"I am not a *cholo*," Slater said through his teeth.

"You can't just hit me."

"You'll take it and you'll like it." Slater slapped him again, landing a single blow before the guy managed to shove him away.

"Break it up," the defense attorney said, and reached across Slater's chest, his forearm on his pecs, gently restraining him. It was a reflexive move, performed as if he'd done it many times before.

The prosecutor waved an arm. "You know this place is crawling with deputies."

"Conveniently for me," Slater said, "None of them are within view right now."

"You assaulted me," he said, raising his voice.

"So you say." Slater clapped the defense attorney on the shoulder. "Take it up with my lawyer."

Turning away, Slater walked out, and down the courthouse steps, into the little park fronting some of the government buildings in downtown Los Angeles.

He paused to look over the sycamores. They'd put in a lot of them here, among the patches of lawn, the pink tables and benches, the boxed dryland plantings. It wasn't a bad idea, as they were natives, but they needed to have a plan to keep the blight and the borers off them. He stepped close to one and examined the bark. So far they looked healthy.

A woman approached him from the direction of the courthouse. He'd seen her inside a minute ago, hovering not far from his conversation with the lawyers. Slater had noticed her when he'd scanned the corridor for deputies before he schooled the prosecutor. She wore her blond hair tied back, and a gray suit that flattered her curves. It looked like standard office drag. Another attorney, maybe, or someone ordered to show up to give testimony like him.

"What's wrong with the tree?" she said as she stepped up.

"Nothing. That's what makes it remarkable." Slater looked her over. "What do you need, sister?"

"My name is Mary-Alice. I heard in there what you do. Investigating people. It sounds like you can get results. Maybe you can help me. It's concerning my ex-husband."

"I'm not going to talk business in the middle of Grand Park, with all these judicial-system lowlifes around. You can come to my office. I'll be there this afternoon."

Slater dug his business card out of his hip pocket and handed it to her, then walked away.

"It's not far from here," she called after him. "I'll be there soon."

He kept walking, not willing to expend the energy

to turn around and explain that he knew how far it was, and that he didn't actually care where she went. But she could be a paying client, and work had been slow—he'd almost considered getting into it with the defense attorney to take on some of those penny-ante subpoena deliveries. On the way to the parking lot he texted his business partner, Max:

> Can you sit in on a new client interview today? At the office. Might be a window-shade job for you.

Max didn't mind the boy-girl stuff, people who wanted them to spy on their cheating spouses, but Slater avoided those jobs. Mostly it felt like they wanted to punish people for having sex, and that felt irrational.

When he descended the stairs into the subterranean parking structure, Slater didn't have to look for his car, as it was hard to miss, a sleek black '78 Thunderbird, a behemoth compared to the auto industry's contemporary bland and uniform offerings. It wasn't always optimal to have a ride that stood out, but he loved it, loved the throaty engine, the classic lines, the cherry interior.

As he climbed in behind the wheel, his phone buzzed, and he pulled it out to check. It was Max's reply:

> I'm here already.

He nosed the Thunderbird up to the street and drove the short distance to their office, in a hundred-year-old high-rise in the Fashion District. Originally an office building, today it was mostly clothing factories. Hustling across the street from the surface parking lot, Slater found a few day laborers still hanging around the lobby, waiting for gig work sewing or cutting or carting garments. Riding up to the ninth floor, he walked around behind the elevator shaft and admired their names on the door:

SLATER IBÁÑEZ
MAXIMILLIAN CONROY
INVESTIGATIONS

Stepping inside, Slater clicked his tongue to greet the little plaster statue of Rey Pascual that sat on the front desk. A skeleton holding a scythe and wearing a crown, Rey's bony empty eye sockets kept watch on the front door. Besides the front office, there was a small one for him, recently painted turquoise to freshen things up, and one for Max, redone in warm yellow.

In Max's office, the only one with a window, he found him sitting behind his desk, wearing a dress shirt with a yellow necktie. His grid-patterned gray suit jacket hung on the coatrack, leaving his holster and the butt of his weapon visible under his arm. Beefy and with mousy brown hair, it was hard to mistake Max for anything other than what he was—the heavy. Slater regularly wanted to punch him in the face, but Max had a PI license, and that gave him access to resources that he wouldn't have on his own. Plus he trusted the guy, and that was worth a lot.

Max leaned back in his chair. "Who's the client?"

"I think it's about bed games," Slater said. "If so, it's all yours. She waylaid me outside the courtroom after she heard me testify about that investigation."

"Are you done on the witness stand?"

"I think so. Let me move one of your guest chairs into my office."

Slater lifted it and carried it over. The recent redecoration had replaced their utilitarian rented office furniture with vintage art deco chairs and desks. Along with the bold colors on the walls after ages of the landlord's flat white, these were a definite upgrade.

Max followed him into his office, shrugging on his suit jacket. "Put it in front of the safe. Maybe she won't notice what it is."

"Good idea," Slater said, and set down the chair.

The less people knew about the safe, the better—it was an antique, and weighed a ton, and was securely bolted to the floor, but it was stuffed with cash. Lots of clients paid them that way, to maintain their anonymity and to avoid leaving a paper trail, and the greenbacks accumulated faster than he and Max could run them through the banks.

There was a sharp knock at the door.

"This one doesn't tarry," Max said. "What's her name?"

"Mary-Alice."

TWO

S LATER STEPPED INTO THE front office to pull open the door, with Max close behind him. Mary-Alice was still in her dour gray suit, a satchel on a long strap slung over her shoulder.

"I wasn't sure I had the right place," she said. "This building is all sewing factories."

"That helps us keep our heads down."

"Mary-Alice, I'm Max," he said, and extended his hand.

"You remembered my name." She smiled and gave Max's big meat hook a gentle shake. "You two really are on the ball." She gestured to the statue on the front desk. "Is this the cartel saint?"

"That's different," Slater said. "This is Rey Pascual. He's from Central America. He's supposed to bring us luck."

"Why is he wearing a crown?"

"Because he's the king of the graveyard. Come in,"

Slater said, and stepped into his office, and behind his desk.

Max extended his arm for Mary-Alice to go first, and she sat in the chair facing Slater's desk. "Is that a safe? I've only seen ones like that in old cartoons."

"It's definitely old-school," Max said, and sat in front of it. "We don't use it for payroll the way a business would have a hundred years ago, but it's useful to secure our confidential files."

Mary-Alice nodded. "I appreciate you meeting with me, Mr. Ibáñez."

"Don't call me that," Slater said. "It makes you sound like all those dirtbags in the justice system. It's just Slater. Are you one of them? Why were you in that courtroom?"

"I work for the oil company. You might have noticed my boss—silk suit, flashy watch. I'm his personal assistant. He was scheduled to testify right after you, but they bumped him to Monday. I think your testimony ran longer than they planned."

Slater nodded. "So what can we help you with?"

"It's about my ex-husband. His name is Harold."

"Personally I don't do boy-girl stuff," Slater said, "but Max here specializes in window-shade jobs."

Mary-Alice scowled. "It's not about peeping in windows. It's our child. I think Harold is endangering her. I need evidence of that to petition for full custody."

"Right now you have joint custody?" Max said.

"That's the agreement."

"An informal agreement," Max said, "or court-ordered?"

She frowned. "A judge decided."

"Why do you think your kid is in danger?" Slater said.

"Rose is just eleven months old. A baby is too much for Harold. He only takes her to spite me. When he brings her home she's cranky and has a two-day load in her diaper. It gives her a terrible rash. I've also seen bruises on her arms."

"Bruises are evidence of abuse," Max said. "You should take that to the county."

Mary-Alice sat up. "I can't prove anything. I need you to do that. Get photos, if you can, and at the very least make a statement about him neglecting the child."

"I guess I can look into it," Slater said. "I'll need a grand to get started. I'll bill you for the rest of my time when I make the report."

"Are you both going to work on it?" she said.

Max waved a hand. "Slater is the lead on your case. He'll pull me in if he needs help."

She flipped open her satchel. "I've got six hundred in cash. Can I write you a check for the rest?"

"Six will work for now," Slater said.

"Your statement will have to be in writing, and on letterhead," Mary-Alice said, and set the C-notes on the desktop.

Slater pulled the bills closer. "What days does Harold have the kid?"

"He's taking her this Saturday for the whole day."

He pulled a yellow pad out of his desk drawer, and a ballpoint pen, and started to make notes.

"Where does he sleep?"

"Harold lives in South LA. He has an apartment on Gage, near Western." She recited the address.

"Does he keep the kid there?"

"I assume so."

"Where does he work?" Slater said.

"At an auto repair shop on Vermont. It's somewhere in the nineties. I don't know the name. I have it in some paperwork at home. I'll text it to you later."

"What kind of car does he drive?"

"A red one."

Slater's eyes narrowed. "Do you know the make, or the plate number?"

"No idea. It's old, though. He's had that car forever. He calls it his taco." She mimicked a deep voice: "'Let me park my taco.' It has a white toolbox in the back, right behind the cab."

"So it's a pickup. Where is it parked when he's at his apartment?"

"He has to park it on the street. It's usually on Gage, except for street-sweeping. I think that's Tuesday morning." She frowned. "Why do you need to know about his car? Are you going to put a tracker on it?"

Slater didn't look up from his note-taking. "Don't ask me that."

"It's usually better if the client doesn't have the full run-down of our techniques," Max said, gesturing widely. "It's called plausible deniability. If your ex-husband ever made you sit for a deposition, or you wound up on the stand in court like Slater today, you can honestly say, 'I don't know what those guys did. I just asked them to get some information.'"

"I understand." Mary-Alice sighed. "Such a seedy world you work in."

"And yet you people keep coming to us," Slater

said, and lifted the stack of C-notes, and waved them at her.

"We do the ugly work so that you don't have to, Mary-Alice," Max said. "You can rest assured that we'll get to the bottom of this."

"Have you got a photo of Harold?" Slater said.

"I'll text it to you."

"Do you send anything along with the kid? Her clothes, maybe?"

"Harold always takes the diaper bag. That has Rose's clothes in it. I put her food in there too."

"What's the bag made of?"

"It's beige." Her brow furrowed. "Canvas, maybe, or that heavy nylon that kind of looks like canvas."

"I'll need to take a look at that before you send it with him."

"You want to put a bug inside?"

"You don't need to know, remember?" Slater said. "Can you bring the bag to your office tomorrow?"

"My boss is headed out of town, so I'll be working from home."

"Where do you live?"

"Vernon."

Slater frowned. "Nobody lives in Vernon. It's all factories and warehouses."

"It's actually Vernon adjacent," she said. "If I tell people Redondo Junction, they think I mean Redondo Beach."

"I thought Redondo Junction was a train yard."

"If you're coming to visit, I guess you'll see for yourself." She stood up and looped the strap of her satchel across her shoulder.

Max rose with her. "I can't believe there's no ring

on that finger, Mary-Alice. How have you managed to stay single?"

She flashed a smile. "I'm a single mother, holding down two jobs, with a vicious ex-husband. But you're very sweet to ask."

Max followed her to the door, and Slater heard him close it after her. He leaned back in his chair and spoke when Max reappeared.

"Thick as peanut butter."

"What are you talking about?" Max said.

"You know exactly what I'm talking about. You lay your mack down, and straight women swoon."

He chuckled. "Not always, but it worked a little with her. She left happy."

"You're so much better with people than I am."

"It's just a different skill."

"Except you can knock heads together the same as I do," Slater said, "but I never got the counterbalance. Those play-nice skills."

"I know you can fake it when you have to."

Slater cocked his head. "So is she running bunco?"

"It's hard to say. To me it feels like it's all roast beef under the gravy. But lots of lowlifes can pull off that act."

"She didn't use the big eye on either of us," Slater said, "even though you opened that door."

"Do you think you're going to need me on this?"

"It seems unlikely. I appreciate you sitting in."

"All part of the deal, buddy," Max said, and carried the extra chair back to his office.

Slater spent a minute typing up his notes on his computer, then called good-bye to Max as he walked out. Once he was down in the parking lot, he fired up the Thunderbird and drove through downtown toward his house in Echo Park. Living there was so new to him that he still had to focus on what streets to take.

Pike should be done with his workday by now. Sweet foxy Pike. Just anticipating being with him made him smile. They were getting pretty sticky, him and Pike, to the point that Slater thought about him all the freaking time, and felt all optimistic when he woke up in the morning. He wanted to be a better man for the guy. He'd been to Pike's place in Albuquerque, and had met some of his people, but he was able to work remotely sometimes, so it was mostly Pike commuting to LA for a few days at a time.

Turning onto his hilly street, Slater pulled up to the boxy modern structure, one of several new interlopers in the historic neighborhood, and pulled into his garage. One flight up was a pair of bedrooms, and the floor above that was the kitchen and a big open room, and beyond it the deck.

Slater climbed the stairs, and walked through the kitchen and the empty space, and stepped out the French doors. It was a cool winter day but the sun made it tolerable, and Pike was stretched out on a lounger with his laptop. He'd positioned it so he'd have a view of the office towers of the Financial District, their top floors visible in the hazy distance.

Thick and a little flabby, with lush dark hair, Pike was wearing chinos and a plaid shirt. He looked up and flashed that smile, brilliant like a spotlight, the look that made Slater's heart soar.

"How's work?" Slater said.

"I can be finished."

He folded his computer closed, and stood up, and wrapped his arms around him. Slater squeezed back and buried his nose in his hair. The scent of his sweat and the warmth of his body were intoxicating. Pike met his mouth, and they got lost in it.

Eventually Pike pulled back and took hold of Slater's necktie, loosening the knot.

"It's so odd to see you dressed like this. How did you do on the stand?"

"It was routine. I'm more interested in this." Slater slapped his butt. "I haven't seen you all day."

Pike chuckled and nuzzled his neck. "I've been thinking about you too."

"I suspect we need to address that," he said, and led him inside, and down to his bedroom.

Slater used the one that faced the street, even though the back bedroom was quieter. He yanked the drapes open to get more light.

Pike already had his shirt off, and Slater pulled the knot out of his tie and unbuttoned his own, and dropped it on the floor, then shoved down his flimsy dress pants. Pike was naked now too, and he climbed onto the bed, and squeezed Slater's cock. Slater kissed his neck, and pulled him close, and met his mouth.

"You're rock-hard," Slater said, stroking him. "You should fuck me."

Pike turned to the bedside table and grabbed a condom and lube. Slater took the little packet, and ripped it open, and rolled it on him.

"Lie on your belly," Pike said, and once Slater had flipped over, he caressed his back, and his butt. "God, I love your ass."

He gently probed him with lubed fingers, then

straddled him, and penetrated him. Slater winced at the intensity of it, shifting position to work with him, and gradually got into it. Thrusting harder, Pike shoved his arms under Slater's, and lowered his weight onto him, and held him tight. He could feel Pike's hot breath on his neck.

With a yelp, Pike thrust deeper as he climaxed, then held him a moment longer before he pulled away.

Slater rolled onto his side, and Pike leaned close, stroking his cock. Slater put his hand on his head and pulled him in, and mouthed his neck and his jaw, and probed his mouth. Inhaling the scent of Pike's sweaty hair, he came, grabbing his hand to make him stop.

Slater rolled onto his back, lifting his head briefly as Pike shifted his arm under his neck. This was the best feeling, these moments, when he was thoroughly sated and spent and relaxed. He closed his eyes and dozed.

Once his breathing had slowed, Pike spoke. "I don't want to leave."

"We still have a few hours," Slater said. "You know we haven't really discussed sex."

"Why would we have to talk about it? We do it pretty regularly."

"I mean about exclusivity. It comes up in my work sometimes. Opportunities to use sex as a tool. I don't want to be limited."

There was no response, and Slater turned to look at him. Pike's brow was furrowed, his gaze sharp.

"Well, that sucks," Pike said finally. "I want you all to myself."

"In my heart there's only you." Slater held his

gaze. "I love you. You know that."

"But you want to fuck other people." Pike sighed. "I guess you did steal a horse and a handgun to come and rescue me, even though I didn't need rescuing."

"I rented the horse, and borrowed the weapon. But that does serve as unimpeachable evidence of how much I'm into you. Unfortunately the dick is separate from the heart."

"Another convoluted thread in our narrative complex."

Slater chuckled and caressed his belly. Early on he'd told someone that their romance was too intricate and complicated to be called a mere story, that it was more appropriate to label it a narrative complex. Since then the term had stuck.

"Is it just that Andy guy?" Pike said. "I could probably deal with that."

"Andy's losing interest in me. I think he's getting tight with his affluent zombie boyfriend. His name is Kyle. That guy is like a vanilla cupcake made flesh. He looks all sweet, but when you're done with him, your teeth hurt and you feel nauseous. It kind of feels like they might go exclusive."

"Exclusive," Pike said. "Huh. There's an interesting word."

"I'm not saying I can't do that." Slater hesitated. "Do you want me to do that?"

"If I asked you to be exclusive, you'd feel hobbled, and you'd start to resent me. Then you'd break it off."

"That's not going to happen."

Pike scowled. "Let me think about it. I can't be rational right now, with your spunk all over me."

"I hate to do this to you."

"I guess the bloom is off the rose."

Pike got up and went into the bathroom. Lying there staring at the ceiling, Slater heard the shower go on. He hated this part—the expectations, the negotiation, the bullshit. Why couldn't it just be good all the time?

Once they were both dressed, Slater in his usual jeans and boots, and they'd eaten some leftovers from the takeout containers in the icebox, Pike carried his little black suitcase down to the garage and loaded it into the backseat of the Thunderbird. As the garage door rolled up, Slater put LAX into the navigation app on his phone, and set it in its dash mount, then backed into the street.

"It's sending me part of the way on surface streets," he said, eyeing the screen. "The 110 must be jammed."

"Why do you call it the 110?" Pike said. "Why not the interstate, or I-110?"

"Because it's not a fucking interstate," Slater snapped. "Or part of it is, and other parts of it aren't. Doris said the freeways were here long before the interstates were invented. Why would we change the damn names? Because the rest of the country caught up to us? You can spare me your Midwestern mores."

Pike chuckled. "I know why you're pissed. I know it's not about freeway names. It's because I'm leaving."

"You're getting to know me pretty well," he said, glancing at him sidelong. "Is that a red flag?"

"The misdirected frustration? Not even a little. I love you, Slater. I love all of you."

Low clouds had rolled in along the coast, he saw as they approached the airport, and soon they were crawling along the snarl of congested roadways toward Pike's terminal. He'd heard talk of rain today. Maybe this was it, moving in from the water. It never freaking rained anymore, but if it was going to happen, it happened in winter.

They shared a last extended kiss in the front seat, and Pike climbed out, and flipped the seat back ahead to pull out his bag. Slater watched for a moment as he towed it into the terminal, then nosed back into the traffic. As he merged onto the 105 he had to turn on the wipers, as the rain had begun.

The steady thrum of rainfall followed him the rest of the way back downtown, and he slowed way down to exit the freeway and to make turns. The roads got slick with the first precipitation of the season, after months of baked-on oil drips and skid marks and urban grime.

Once he was upstairs in the kitchen, he could actually hear the muffled drumming of the raindrops striking the flat roof overhead. Hopefully it wasn't going to leak, he thought, surveying the ceiling. Flat roofs were notorious for that. This was the first time it had rained since he'd been in this house.

Pulling one of the fifths of bourbon from the pantry cupboard, Slater poured his ration into a tumbler. Under his booze rules he was only allowed half an inch, but it usually wound up being a little more, closer to an inch, what with his heavy hand. Still, he'd come up with the rules for a reason—he needed to be in control of it, even when Pike wasn't around to behave for.

He took the first delicious sip, relishing the heat in his nose and his throat. Already he could feel the warmth in his belly, making the world begin to slow down. The only furniture in the big room, between the kitchen and the deck, was a living room set with a TV, positioned at one side near the French doors. He carried the tumbler over to the sofa and set it on the floor, and stretched out, and looked at his phone.

There'd been texts from Mary-Alice—her ex's work address, and a couple of photos of him. Harold had shaggy African hair and a bit of stubble on his face. He was thick—a little overweight, maybe, but he looked built. In one of the photos he was standing with her, both of them smiling. Harold was almost a head taller than she was. The guy looked like a bruiser, and he was totally fuckable.

Slater took a gulp of the amber elixir and set his phone face down on the floor. He wasn't quite sure yet what to make of Mary-Alice. But he could think about it tomorrow. Right now the warm glow was suffusing his body, slowing things down, unspooling his mind.

THREE

SLATER'S ALARM SOUNDED WELL before dawn, and he forced himself out of bed, shivering in the cold air, and pulled on his jeans and a collared shirt and a lightweight jacket. Bleary-eyed, he decided to forgo coffee, and trotted down to his garage.

Past the nose of the Thunderbird was a tall cabinet, built to look like a basic tan sheet-metal box from an office-supply store. In reality it was a heavily armored gun safe, bolted to the concrete floor, with a serious multipoint lock on it. Slater didn't have any firearms, but he kept his illicit gear inside, mostly the stuff he acquired from the Russians in Glendale.

Once he had it open, he pulled a vehicle tracker off its charger. About the size of a cell phone, but a little thicker, it was an unmarked black box with rib magnets studding one side. Relocking the cabinet, he climbed into the Thunderbird and waited for the garage door to roll up.

The rain was finished, but even in the dark he could see the pavement was still wet. Slater flicked on his headlights and followed the navigation app onto the 110. Traffic was light so early in the morning, and he sped south toward Harold's place, the Thunderbird purring comfortably in its natural environment, and soon exited onto surface streets.

As he came up on the address, the only red pickup in view was a Tacoma, parked under a streetlight. He slowed down as he passed it. The plates were old, with the embossed version of CALIFORNIA, before they switched to the printed-on version. That dated the vehicle to the early 1990s. There was a white toolbox in the bed, and the badge on the rear gate had been rearranged to read MA TACO. That made him smile. Whether the letters had fallen off and Harold had put them back on that way, or he'd actually bothered to pry off the badge and split the letters, it was funny. Mary-Alice said he called the vehicle his taco, and that it was old—this had to be Harold's ride.

Slater parked the Thunderbird farther up the block and killed the lights. It took a second to find the tiny power switch on the side of the vehicle tracker, and he clicked it on with a fingernail. Reaching into the backseat, he grabbed a pair of black latex gloves from the box he kept there, and wriggled his hands into them, then palmed the tracker and climbed out. As he strode back toward the pickup, he rubbed the tracker on his thigh to wipe off his fingerprints. His DNA was still all over it, of course, but it was unlikely any investigation would go that deep.

When he walked up on the vehicle he slowed his pace. In the dark interior, he saw that a car seat was mounted on the passenger side. Stepping behind the Tacoma and into the street, he squatted next to the rear wheel. It was still too early for traffic, with only a couple of vehicles passing since he'd pulled up, so he could work unobserved. The car was wet from the rain, and as he reached up inside the wheel well, he could feel the water soak in through the arm of his jacket.

The task went quickly—with the vehicle's high clearance there was lots of room to maneuver, and the magnetic ribs on the device quickly found steel to attach to. It didn't need a view of the sky because it didn't use GPS signals from space, instead sniffing out much stronger terrestrial Wi-Fi and cell signals to send to the Russians' software to calculate its general location. It was less precise, but the big advantage was that it used much less power than a GPS receiver— this thing would broadcast its position for days.

Walking back to his car, he saw the faint glow of twilight looming on the eastern horizon. He could have done this last night, but it was a crowded neighborhood, and there would have been too many people around. The hours before dawn were usually the quietest.

And yet here was someone out on the sidewalk. A dark-skinned bald guy wearing a sweatshirt, standing with a tiny Chihuahua at the end of a leash, the dog sniffing around on the verge. He eyed Slater as he approached.

"What's the gloves for?"

He'd forgotten about those—he should have already taken them off. Not pausing, Slater growled, "Spread out."

"It's a simple question," he called after him. "Why is your arm all wet?"

Ignoring him, Slater kept walking. The guy hadn't seen anything. He was brave to confront him like that, out on his own, even if he was the neighborhood-watch type. Someone more impulsive than Slater would have gut-punched him.

The drive back to his house went fast, as most people still weren't up. Stripping off his clothes, he yanked the drapes closed and climbed into bed.

Hours later, when he got up again, his head hurt, and he felt a little groggy. He sent Svetlana a text:

Can I come by today?

Her reply came before he'd even finished dressing:

You know where to find me.

Upstairs he ate some dry toast, and a mugful of the cold java that still sat in the pot from yesterday's breakfast with Pike, then went down to the garage and drove toward the freeway.

The streets were drying out in the morning sun, and when he pulled up at Svetlana's building, in a seedy part of Glendale, the new foliage in front of her workshop looked vibrant and freshly rinsed. The city would be happy, as the ivy and fast-growing trees were almost completely covering the run-down facade they'd complained to her about. When Svetlana had asked him for help with it, he'd recommended someone else to do the work, a colleague from his horticulture days who was still in the game. She'd clearly aced the plantings.

The entrance on this side of the building, facing

the street, looked like it hadn't been used in years. Knowing Svetlana it was probably nailed shut. He walked around to the alley, and pressed the buzzer next to the back door, then looked up into the overhead camera and double-clicked his tongue.

The door buzzed, and he pulled it open, and stood in the dark anteroom for a moment while the machinery silently scanned him for weapons. Eventually the inner door snapped open, and he stepped inside.

The interior of the workshop was always dimly lit, with long workbenches littered with electronics and plastic casings and tools. Svetlana was here alone today, perched on her stool at her computer, her bulky frame clad in a red skirt and a blouse printed with colorful pansies. In her fifties, she had some weight on her frame, and wasn't afraid to show some cleavage. She swiveled to greet him as he stepped in.

"This boyfriend that I met," Svetlana said, her Slavic accent flattening the vowels. "Mr. Pike. What agency does he work for?"

It was a little worrisome that she remembered his name, Slater thought. They'd only been in the same room for a hot minute, but she'd quickly made him as a fed.

"ATF," he said, "but they loan him out to other agencies."

"So he's working with guns and explosives. That's not something I usually do."

"He's never going to know anything about you. I told him you help me with security. He knows you installed my heavy-duty garage door, but that's it."

"Can you ask him for access to information?"

"From his job?" Slater slowly shook his head. "I don't want to do that. I need to keep him out of my work."

"Perhaps you have some personal information about him."

He laughed. "You think I should blackmail my own boyfriend?"

"Nothing so criminal. But sensitive information can be used as leverage."

"Pike is on the up-and-up. I've never seen him do anything that would qualify as leverageable."

She shrugged. "I had to ask. Federal databases could be an extremely valuable resource."

"I don't think he'd do it for love nor money."

"*Zechote.* I get it. So what do you need today?"

"A camera," Slater said, and explained the surveillance he needed to do with the diaper bag.

"Why not get two cameras? One for either side of this bag. Then you always have a view."

"That's a great idea."

Svetlana slid off her stool and stepped over to the door into the next room, tapping her wrist to the sensor mounted next to it. It unlocked with a snap, and she stepped through. Someone else was working over there, he realized, as Svetlana spoke in Russian, and he heard a woman's voice respond before she pulled the door closed behind her.

Some of her employees were definitely family. When he'd started working with her, Svetlana had been in a partnership, with her brother Igor. He'd been away for a long time on what Svetlana had framed as a pointless personal quest in Russia's far east. His absence didn't matter for Slater's purposes;

Svetlana was perfectly capable of doing the business's heavy lifting on her own.

A minute later she returned with a handful of stuff. Two foil-wrapped flat packs, a few inches square, he saw as she handed him one. They looked like they might be soft, like a slice of rye bread wrapped in kitchen foil, but each was firm and inflexible.

"Most of the volume is the battery." She pointed out a black component in the middle of one side. "The lens is in this pinhole."

"These are thin. They should work great."

"Use this to secure it." She gave him a couple of black fabric swatches, a little larger than the camera pack. "This side has glue. Peel off the liner and it will stick to the inside of the bag to hold the camera in place. It should broadcast for four days."

"Clearly you've thought this through."

"A customer wanted a camera to wear inside his jacket," she said. "It's the same as what you need. I'll connect them to your account."

Climbing on her stool again, she spent a minute tapping at her keyboard, then scanned the bar-code label on each flat pack with the glowing red tip of a wand that was wired to her computer. From where Slater was standing, the screen was a fuzzy blur—she had a privacy filter on it. She peeled the little label off each unit, then put them in a paper grocery bag along with the squares of black fabric.

"Have you heard about facial recognition software?" Svetlana swiveled toward him.

"I know what it is, but I don't know much about it."

"The police are using it. Quietly, of course. More

important, the online data-broker companies are selling records of all the faces that they pick up on security cameras. They buy footage from anyone who has cloud storage cameras."

"Selling them to who?"

"Anyone. Law enforcement, government agencies, even consumer websites."

"I guess it's impossible not to be recognized," Slater said, "unless you go around in a ski mask."

Scooping up a pair of eyeglasses that were sitting under the desk lamp on her workbench, she handed them to him.

"These are heavy." Slater turned them over and folded the arms open. They had thick frames with a weird multicolored pattern, and the lenses were flat.

"It's the batteries. Always the batteries. They're in the arms." She leaned toward him and pointed to the front of the frames. "Do you see the spots?"

There were little pits spaced evenly around both lenses, he saw.

"Those are UV and IR lamps. The human eye can't see the light, but they will wash out your face on many security cameras. I'll show you."

She turned back to her computer and waved him closer. When he stood just behind her shoulder, the screen went clear. She pulled up a video, with a familiar face in the frame—Svetlana's nephew Garik. He was sitting on a stool, in this room, looking at the camera. He said something in Russian, then picked up a pair of glasses like the ones Slater was holding, and examined one of the arms. Suddenly a brilliant white glare surrounded them, blurring his hands. When Garik pulled them on, all that was visible was his chin—most of his face was obscured in blue-white light. He waved his hand in front of his face, and said something else in Russian, and the video ended.

"That's totally genius," Slater said. "Was this your idea?"

She swiveled to face him and shrugged. "I stand on the shoulders of giants."

Slater held the glasses up to the overhead fluorescent fixture. The lenses had a blueish cast, but they didn't distort the view the way prescription glasses did.

"In daylight, or if the camera can filter the UV, the design on the frame will throw off some of the software programs that try to match your face," Svetlana said. "The pattern adds mathematical confusion, so the software will create an entry for a new person. It won't be connected to the entry for your face the way it looks without the glasses."

"Of course I have to have a pair of these."

She chuckled. "Special price for a regular customer. Three dollars. Bring them back sometimes and I'll swap them for a pair with a different pattern. Each time you change the frames, your face will be registered as a different person."

"Where's the power switch?"

Taking them back, she showed him the little slider under one of the arms, and the charging port on the other arm.

"The indicator turns green when the battery is full."

"How often do I need to charge them?"

"Think of it like your phone. Every day or so."

Slater pulled out his wad of cash and paid her for the cameras and the glasses.

"There's no guarantee you won't be recognized," Svetlana said, handing him the paper bag, "especially if a human is involved in reviewing the footage. But it will slow down the automated systems."

"I'll say it again, Svetlana—you're a genius."

She beamed and waved dismissively.

Walking out to the alley, and around to his car, he had to grin. She still trusted him with her cutting-edge stuff—the new glasses—even though he was dating a fed. That was very good news.

When he punched Mary-Alice's address into his navigation, it led him into the industrial zone south of downtown, just beyond the 10. The streets were lined with warehouses, fronted by chain-link fences topped with razor wire, the long windowless walls covered with graffiti and mismatched color swatches where the tagging had been painted over. That rail yard had to be right around here. Turning onto her street, he rolled past an ugly container lot and parked along a cinderblock wall. There was no sidewalk, just weeds and trash along the wall. Could this really be where she lived?

Climbing out of the car, he saw that the ancient uneven asphalt was drying out, but the parts in the shade of the structures were still wet. He scanned the block, but there were no numbers on the buildings. Across the street a chemical-hazard placard caught his eye. Mounted next to a heavy steel door, it was an altered version of the real one, with an *A* at the top instead of numbers—an artist worked here, not toxic chemicals.

Slater walked over and banged on the door. A minute later Mary-Alice pulled it open, holding a baby in one arm.

"I thought you worked for an oil company," Slater said. "You have the artist symbol on your door."

"My neighbor is the artist, not me." She beckoned him to follow her in.

It was a hallway with a couple of other doors, he saw, and Mary-Alice led him through the one that hung open. Inside was a little bubble of residential space. It felt like a loft, and it was mostly unfinished, with some wallboard installed but mostly raw framing. Colorful wire and ventilation ducts looped over the open rafters, and the inner surface of the curved roof was visible higher above. There was no bed in sight— it must be through the interior doorway. In this room was a kitchen table and a sofa and a TV, with a big industrial sink and a counter along one wall. A bar fridge sat below it, and there was a microwave on top.

"This neighborhood is all about diesel trucks," Slater said, looking around. "I hope you have good air filtration."

Mary-Alice was focused on the baby in her arms. "This is Rose."

The kid looked at him with big brown eyes.

"Here," Mary-Alice said, handing her toward him. "Hold her."

"I don't think that's necessary."

"You should."

Slater stifled a sigh and grasped the kid under her arms. She was able to hold her own head up—he knew that was important when you were handling babies.

"How you doing, kid?" Slater bounced her up and down a little.

"You can see what the stakes are," Mary-Alice said.

The kid smiled a little, in that way babies did, her entire face contorting, showing her little gums and a couple of nubby teeth.

"I think she wants to go back to you," Slater said. "She looks nervous."

"She's fine. She likes you."

"OK, then, I'm the one who's nervous. By definition, tiny people are extremely fragile."

Mary-Alice took the kid back, setting her on her shoulder and gently patting her back.

Slater put his hands on his hips. "You didn't tell me Harold was black."

"He's kind of black, and kind of a mutt. Does it matter?"

"It reduces the array of tools I can use. I can't get him involved with law enforcement. If he was white I could use the cops against him."

She frowned. "You think the cops are just itching to shoot black guys."

"It doesn't matter what I think. Ask a black guy."

"So what is it that you want to do to the diaper bag?"

"Remember plausible deniability?" he said. "Where's the bag?"

Mary-Alice nodded toward the kitchen table, and Slater stepped over to it. The bag was squat, and made of heavy tan-colored nylon, with a big handle on the top. It had backpack straps too. Scuffed and worn and stained in places, it looked well used.

"I'm going to take it out to my car for a few minutes," he said, and lifted it off the table. "Christ, do you carry bricks around in this thing?"

"It's all things for Rose. Babies are complicated."

Slater took it out to the street, and grabbed his toolbox from the trunk of the Thunderbird, then climbed in behind the wheel. He set the toolbox on the floor and the diaper bag on the passenger seat. One of the cameras would go on the side opposite the backpack straps, he decided, pulling them out of the paper bag, and one would go right between the straps. Even though Harold might wear it like a backpack, some of the time it would be sitting on a table, like it had been at Mary-Alice's, or on a chair, or on the floor.

Flipping open the toolbox, he found an awl, then zipped open the bag's outermost pouch and made a hole in the fabric. Once he'd lined it up with the lens of Svetlana's flat camera, he pressed the fabric patch over it, glad that the adhesive stuck firmly. It looked a little bulky with the zipper open, but hopefully Harold wouldn't notice. The hole for the lens wasn't noticeable either, among the snags and stains and marks on the fabric.

The opposite side, between the straps, was harder to access, and he had to haul out a bunch of diapers and a blanket to get to the right spot. Once he had the camera installed and taped in place, he packed them all in again.

On his phone he pulled up Svetlana's app and looked for the cameras. They were both working— one showed the inside of the Thunderbird's passenger door, and the other was a view of his own torso and the steering wheel.

Stowing the toolbox in the trunk again, he carried the bag back to Mary-Alice's door and banged on it.

"Where's the kid?" he demanded when she pulled it open.

"Taking a nap." She eyed the diaper bag. "So is this bugged now?"

"No comment." He handed it to her. "Make sure Harold takes it with him tomorrow. I'll be in touch."

FOUR

ACK IN HIS CAR, Slater looked at his phone and tapped on the live stream for the cameras. One of them was trained on the floor, and the other showed Mary-Alice's face looking down at the lens, her brow furrowed, the loft's rafters visible behind her. Then the view dropped to floor level, and with a dull *clunk* both frames went black. She'd put it in a cupboard—Mary-Alice didn't want to be bugged.

While he had Svetlana's software open, he looked at the map for the location tracker on Harold's pickup. It was still parked outside his apartment. Next he checked on the location of his idiot ex-boyfriend, Conrad. Back when they'd been together Slater had surreptitiously put tracking software on his phone. It wasn't stalking, he reasoned, as he needed to know where the guy was sometimes. But today it gave him a message he'd never seen before—instead of the usual dot on the map it said "разъед."

Svetlana was based here, but her software was such a mishmash of English and Russian that he suspected she outsourced the software development to people in the motherland. He didn't know what that word meant, but when he tapped on the location history for Conrad's phone, he saw that it had gone offline midday yesterday. Svetlana's tech never broke down. That meant Conrad had changed something— he'd found the software and deleted it, the drooling moron, or something else had happened. Zooming in on the map for the phone's last known location, he saw that it had been on a boulevard, in a retail space, not far from the station where Conrad worked—a phone store. He dialed his cell number.

When Conrad picked up, Slater said, "Did you get a new phone?"

"How did you know that?"

"Your voice sounds different."

"It was time," Conrad said. "I upgraded."

"Are you at work?"

"Why?"

"I need info on a guy in a case I'm on. I'll text you his name."

"I can't be digging into people's police files," Conrad said. "You know that."

"I don't need his colonoscopy video, or his dick pics. I just need to know if he's a knucklehead or a civilian. Has he done time, has he got a rap sheet, that kind of thing. It's what my taxes pay you to keep track of. I'll text you the name."

"I'm busy," Conrad said, but Slater hung up on him.

Once he'd texted him Harold's name and his

address on Gage, he twisted the key in the ignition, and drove out of the bleak industrial neighborhood, and back to his house. As he waited for the garage door to roll down, he saw that Conrad had texted:

I have updates. Call me.

He must have found details about Harold. It was smart of him not to put it in writing. Slater texted back:

Want to come over for lunch? I haven't seen you in a while.

He climbed the stairs and thought through his plan. He'd give Conrad something caffeinated, and sweet—he liked sugary iced coffee. Then he'd likely have to piss, and he'd probably leave his phone on the table. The fool had dropped one in the john once, destroying it, and that had made him risk-averse about his gadgets. If he used the same unlock code as on his old phone, Slater should have time to install the tracking software on the new device.

Conrad's response came as he got up to the kitchen:

If you're buying, I'll be there soon.

It was that time of day, Slater realized, even though it felt much earlier. His predawn excursion had skewed his sense of time and prematurely tired him out. On his phone he ordered takeout from a Thai place they both used to like, and chose the largest iced coffee they had.

Before long the doorbell rang, and he trotted down to open it. Barrel-chested, with broad shoulders and thick black hair, Conrad flashed that easy smile. Such a beautiful man. He was wearing his work drag—a gray suit and a dark-blue necktie.

"That suit," Slater said, furrowing his brow.

"What's wrong with it?"

"You might as well wear a sandwich board that says 'police detective.'"

Conrad gave him a pointed once-over. "If I dressed like you, I'd need a sandwich board that said 'itinerant gardener.'"

"I'd punch you in the face right now, but the food's here."

A car had stopped in front of the garage door, and Slater stepped over to the passenger window, and grabbed the bag of food, and slipped the guy a fin as a tip. Conrad followed him up the stairs.

"Should we eat here, or on the deck?" Slater said, once they were in the kitchen.

He waved toward the French doors. "It's warm enough out."

Handing him the bag, Slater grabbed forks and plates and followed him outside.

"It always smells so clean after it rains," Conrad said, dropping into one of the chairs at the patio table.

"I'm just glad the water isn't pooling anywhere out here. This is the first time it's rained since I moved in."

After they'd eaten, Slater stacked their plates and tucked the empty containers into the bag they'd come in.

"About your man Harold," Conrad said, sitting back. "I think he's a civilian. He's only been arrested once. In a bar, for assault. The charges were dropped."

"Who dropped it—the cops or the prosecutors?"

"We did."

"Do you know why?"

"Sometimes somebody higher up decides there's not enough evidence." Conrad waved a hand. "Sometimes if you're drunk or high they charge you so they can hold you until you dry out, and then they drop it. Sometimes in a brawl they just charge everybody until they can sort out who started it."

"That wasn't laid out in his rap sheet?"

"It happened a while ago. Maybe Harold was legitimately defending himself, or maybe he was just shitfaced." Conrad sipped at the dregs of the big iced coffee. "I should get back to work. Let me hit the head."

He rose and stepped in through the French doors. Exactly as planned, he left his phone on the table. Once he was inside, Slater grabbed it and thumb-typed the unlock code. It worked—he'd used the same one as on his old phone.

"Idiot," he muttered.

On the screen, behind the grid of apps, the background image was a photo of a conifer-studded mountainside. Slater knew that place—Kings Canyon. Conrad had taken this photo. He loved it up there. They'd gone camping together in this very spot. A short hike in from the road, they'd slept on the hard ground, and froze in the middle of the night. Despite the discomfort, he'd actually had a blast, because he'd been with Conrad. Staring at the photo, he wondered if the guy still went up there, still went camping, pitched his tent with other people.

Maybe he didn't need to do this. He pressed the

power button to lock the phone. The screen went dark, and he set it on the table. It would be weird not to have eyes on the guy. But maybe it was time to let go of that.

A minute later Conrad came back, stepping outside with that swagger of his, and shot him a smile.

"It took you long enough," Slater said. "Couldn't you find your dick? I can loan you a magnifying glass."

He scoffed and scooped up his phone. "That's not what you said when you were riding it, cowboy."

Slater grabbed the plates and the plastic bag and carried them inside to the kitchen, then followed him down the stairs.

"It was good to see you," Conrad said, pausing outside the front door. "It looks like you're doing OK."

"Yeah, well, nobody's managed to grease me just yet."

"That's a positive trend. Let's keep it that way. How's it going with the boyfriend?"

"He's in Albuquerque."

"In my job we call that misdirection," Conrad said, and put his hands on his hips. "I asked how it was going, not where he was."

"You're such a cop." He scoffed. "It's actually going pretty freaking great, detective. I feel high all the time. I'm in way over my head, and I don't know what the hell I'm doing, but that feels OK. He doesn't hate me yet."

"I get it. I saw you two together. It made me happy for you."

"Thanks, man."

Conrad's eyes narrowed. "'Thanks'? Are you on

something? Slater Ibáñez doesn't use that word."

"Slater Ibáñez is about to dick-punch you," he said, and jutted his chin. "So you'd best piss off back to wherever you came from."

He guffawed, rolling his head back. "That's more like it."

As he walked toward his car, Slater closed the door. Such a dick-smack. It was like he intentionally wanted to wind him up. Not having eyes on the guy might actually be kind of liberating. Like when he'd moved house and cleaned out the kitchen junk drawer, and organized the shelves in the garage, and downsized his ragtag collection of clothes.

There'd been an alert on his phone a minute ago, and when he looked at it now, he saw that Harold's vehicle had moved. It was on Vermont, way down south. Mary-Alice had said that's where he worked. At an auto repair shop. She'd texted him the address last night.

Climbing into the Thunderbird, he headed south on the freeway, exiting on Manchester. Max called this neighborhood Murdertown. Statistically more people got shot on the streets around their office, but this was a close runner-up. In daylight it wasn't that rough, just poor, the boulevard lined with storefront churches, dollar stores, and an inordinate number of body shops and auto repair joints.

As he cruised past the garage, Slater spotted the red Tacoma, street-parked on the same block. Pulling a U-turn, he drove back to where he could get a view of the place, on the opposite side of the street, and parked at the curb. He grabbed his binoculars from the backseat and trained them on the garage.

The doors on all three bays were rolled up, with a vehicle up on a lift in the middle one. He could see people inside.

Harold, he realized, watching a tall guy in stained blue coveralls move from one bay to the next, carrying a car battery in both hands. He had to be over six feet tall, and thick, like the photos of him had implied. His hair was tucked under a backward ball cap. The vehicle he went to had its hood up and was parked halfway out of the garage bay. He was using the daylight to work on the engine, Slater decided, watching him stoop over it with the battery.

Now that he'd seen the guy, there was really no reason to sit here. Harold wouldn't have the kid with him until tomorrow. But at least he'd learned what he looked like in person, and that he really did have a job. Plus he was stacked, based on the way his overalls fit around his crotch. But that probably wouldn't matter.

Harold straightened up, and arched his back, and rolled his neck, turning his face to the sun. Standing there for a minute, he looked across the street, right at Slater.

Dropping the binoculars, Slater slouched down in his seat. Had the guy made him? Maybe not—his expression unchanged, Harold turned back to the car and leaned into it again. Slater twisted the key in the ignition, and pulled into the street, and drove to his office.

Upstairs he eyed Rey Pascual as he stepped in, and briefly stuck his head into Max's office to make sure he was alone.

"Just you and me, Rey," he said, and went into his own office. There was paperwork to do for their accountant, O'Dowd. She'd been ramping up the pressure on him and Max to provide details of their income and expenses. They mostly got paid in cash, and they'd started smurfing their earnings into the bank, a little each month, so as not to attract a drug-money audit. But O'Dowd insisted she needed income records for each deposit.

At his desk he worked for a few hours, basically making stuff up to explain the cash deposits. All of the dough was their legitimate earnings, but they couldn't out their clients to the tax people, or to anyone else, so the record-keeping required creative flair.

Sometime after six his phone buzzed, and when he checked, he saw that the Tacoma was on the move. It was on the freeway, well past the exit for Harold's place on Gage, headed right toward downtown. Slater locked his computer, and killed the lights, and twisted his key to set the deadbolt as he left. It was dark out, the street quiet, the parking lot abandoned for the day.

Firing up the Thunderbird, he studied his phone screen, watching the green marker that indicated the Tacoma's location shift from point to point. The circle was larger and less precise when a vehicle was moving, sometimes contracting as it found new Wi-Fi stations and Svetlana's software checked their physical coordinates in the public databases. The circle hopped past this neighborhood, just a few streets away, and into Skid Row. Then it stopped moving, and the circle shrank, then shrank again as it gained confidence about its position.

He backed out of the parking space and drove toward Skid Row, just a few blocks north. The neighborhood didn't look that different from where his office was, although the density of the tents lining the sidewalks here was definitely higher. The red Tacoma was street-parked, he saw, in the middle of a block of retail, and as he drove past, he saw that no one was in the cab. Where the hell was Harold? Everything around here was shuttered and closed up tight.

Except one place, he realized, toward the end of the block. It was new construction, a glassy tower looming over the sagging old low-rise neighborhood. The lights were on in the lobby. It had been built as transitional housing for the neighborhood's vast homeless population, and he knew the ground floor had meeting rooms—he'd attended a string of infuriating sessions here himself, his court-ordered anger management classes.

Scowling at the memory, he rounded the corner, and pulled into a street space, then walked back to the building and tried the door. It was unlocked, and he stepped into the lobby. The guy behind the security desk wasn't wearing a uniform, and from his wild hair, bushy beard, and blotchy red skin, he looked like he might still be on the skids. He briefly glanced up at Slater, seemingly unconcerned at his presence.

Walking into the familiar corridor where the meeting rooms were, he found a couple of the doors propped open, others closed. The first one had a paper sign taped to it: AA. The next door was marked 72, whatever the hell that meant, and past that was a closed door marked NA. Twelve-step meetings. It was the right time of day for it, just after work for most people. And after dark was when the greatest temptation pressed its weight down.

Taking a breath, he pulled open the door to the NA meeting. It hadn't started yet, or maybe it had just ended. A dozen people stood around talking. Just a few of the chairs were occupied. These junkies were an array of genders, spanning college age to retirement, and not all of them looked homeless. There was no sign of Harold. A woman standing by the coffee pot caught his eye, and smiled, and beckoned him in.

Ignoring her, he stepped out and pulled the door closed. The AA meeting was in progress, he saw through the half-open door. He slowed his steps as he approached. There was Harold—sitting with his back to the entrance, half a head taller than anyone else, his bundle of hair unmistakable.

Slater walked past and paused for a moment in the lobby. He could go sit in that meeting without attracting attention, as there were a lot of bodies in the room. But the likelihood that Harold would speak seemed slim. If he sat there now it might actually blow his cover with the guy later on. Plus he'd have to listen to all the yapping.

He walked out to the street. Andy was in a similar narcotics recovery group, and he'd met some of those people when he'd dragged Slater to his NA meeting. Andy had been a pill-popper, but the junkies who were on the hard-core illegal dope for very long became thieving lowlifes. AA was milder—it was for drunks, and drunks were usually just boring. They didn't need to steal to maintain their addiction. If Harold was in an AA meeting, maybe he'd kicked the habit.

Headed up the block toward the corner, there weren't many people around, but he felt eyes on him.

A guy with a high forehead and scraggly hair stood at the curb, hands in his jacket pockets, openly watching him approach.

"You holding?" the guy said as he walked past.

"Spread out," Slater said.

"Fricking junkie."

Slater turned back. "I know this is your neighborhood, but why would you say that to me? You're the one trying to buy drugs, and I'm the junkie?"

"You just came out of that NA meeting. I saw you. And you look like a junkie."

Slater took a step toward him and punched him on the chin. The guy quickly struck back, landing a blow on the side of his mouth. He hadn't expected that—he'd assumed he would be too drug-addled to land a blow. But he was fast.

As the guy swung at him again, Slater ducked and delivered a solid dick-punch, then stepped back. He could taste blood in his mouth. The guy groaned and curled in on himself.

"Why do you make me do this to you?" Slater shouted, and kicked him in the ass.

The guy stumbled off the curb but didn't topple over. Slater touched his lip. It was numb, and it was already swelling.

"Idiot," he muttered, and walked away. He hated this neighborhood.

Upstairs at his house, he poured his ration of bourbon into a tumbler, then sloshed in a little extra. He deserved it—he'd gotten punched in the face tonight. Plus Pike wasn't around, so there was less incentive to behave. He didn't hide his consumption from Pike, but he didn't want the guy to think he was an addict either, so he usually tried to go easy.

Tumbler in hand, he went over to the French doors, and probed his injured lip with his tongue. It wouldn't be too bad. Maybe the swelling would be gone by morning. He gazed out at the glittering metropolis and slurped from his glass, relishing the burn in his throat. The frenetic chaos out there was always cranked up to ten. Pugilistic junkies, block-long rows of tents all over town, fully employed people living like squatters in a damn warehouse. The dull roar of it was so constant that he didn't even hear it anymore.

FIVE

Mary-Alice had told him Harold was picking up the kid at eight, and Slater's alarm went off well before that. Looking at the tracking app, he saw that Harold's vehicle was headed east, already on his way to her place. Once he'd set the diaper-bag cameras to record everything, he got dressed, and went upstairs to make coffee, then checked the tracker again.

Harold was headed away from Mary-Alice's now, but he was farther west than his own place. Slater slurped at his java, then hustled down to his car and got on the freeway, keeping an eye on the tracker. The marker stopped, eventually, in the middle of Baldwin Hills. The green circle was wide and imprecise, likely due to the dearth of Wi-Fi stations nearby, but it was unmistakably atop the hills in that undeveloped open space—a public park.

Minutes later he was cruising up the access road into the park. Today it was scrub grassland and a few trees, but Doris said in the twentieth century this had been a reservoir, until the day the dam failed. She remembered watching the torrent of water, with furniture and debris and people's Christmas presents floating down overflowing Ballona Creek.

The red Tacoma was here, in the first parking lot, and Slater nosed the Thunderbird farther up the hill, to the next lot, and pulled into a space. He looped his binoculars around his neck, twisting them back under one arm, then walked on one of the park's dirt paths toward Harold's pickup.

Lots of people were here today, as it was Saturday, and it was warm. Up ahead he spotted Harold, his big frame pushing a stroller, the familiar diaper bag on his back. Wearing jeans and a black T-shirt, his intricate sleeve tats were visible curling around both arms.

Slater followed them at a distance until Harold sat on a bench, pulling the stroller close. He was far enough away that he could watch them without being obvious about it, and he found a bench, and pulled his glasses around, and focused them on Harold. He was leaning into the stroller. From this distance Slater couldn't hear what he was saying, but his lips were moving, and his expression was animated.

Harold lifted out the kid, a bundle in a white blanket, and folded the fabric away from her head. His big hands on her torso, he bounced her up and down on his lap, his lips moving all the while. It looked like he was talking nonstop. The kid seemed content with him, big-eyed, glancing around the park but mostly gazing at him.

After a while he put her back in the stroller,

and got up, and slung the diaper bag onto his back. He pushed the stroller farther up the hill, moving at a leisurely pace, and then wheeled it into a public restroom. Slater followed, walking up the path. When he got to the building, he stepped inside. Harold had the kid laid out on the pull-down changing table, with the diaper bag zipped open. He was singing, and didn't look up as Slater entered.

Stepping over to the sinks, Slater pressed the faucet and rinsed his hands. There were no mirrors, so he couldn't watch them, but Harold was definitely changing her diaper. The song he was singing was "What a Wonderful World." That hadn't been written with babies in mind, but the way Harold was performing it was calm, his tone soft—it wouldn't alarm the kid.

This place was remarkably clean for a public restroom, he realized, walking out into the daylight. Maybe they managed to keep the junkies and the homeless out of it. Maybe that's why Harold came here—it was actually functional.

Some distance farther up the path he found a bench with a view of the restroom, and sat with his binoculars trained on the doorway to watch for Harold to step out.

A body stepped into his field of view and stopped, completely obscuring both lenses. When Slater lowered the glasses, he found a scruffy bearded guy in a heavy jacket, a wry grin on his face, standing a few feet in front of him.

"Move it," Slater snapped.

"For a dollar, I will."

Slater stood up, and stepped over to him, and

punched him on the chin. His head snapped sideways, and Slater took a step back, breathing through his mouth at the sudden tang of homelessness, like vinegar and ammonia and digested booze.

"You can't just hit people," the guy said, eyes wide.

"You can't just shake people down for cash without expecting consequences," Slater said.

"You're a damn bully."

"And you're lucky you smell so bad. Otherwise I'd flatten you. Now, beat it."

In the distance he caught sight of Harold, outside on the path again with the stroller, on the move. The scrounge was still glaring at him as Slater walked away and slung his binoculars under his arm.

Harold wheeled the kid farther up the hill, through a squat red-and-black gate that bore a sign that Slater couldn't read until he was closer: JAPANESE GARDEN. It did kind of look like a torii gate, he realized. Walking in, he saw the stroller parked a few yards away, along the fence that surrounded a placid pond, its surface thick with waterlilies, spanned by a vermilion-red footbridge. The kid was in Harold's arms now, her entire being barely bigger than one of his biceps. Both of them were looking at the water.

A lot of people stood at the railing, giving Slater enough anonymity to walk right behind Harold and the kid, slowing to a casual stroll. As he passed he tried to tune in to Harold's voice.

"The turtles don't live under the water," Harold was saying. "They just like to swim there."

Why would he be telling her that? The kid was too young to glean anything. She'd never retain it.

There were a fuckload of turtles, he realized,

glancing into the pond as he circled it. Some were perched on rocks, but most were under the surface of the water, in places hidden by the waterlilies, where they jostled for space.

Once he'd made the circuit, Slater walked out of that section of the park, back down the path toward the parking lots, and sat on a bench. A while later Harold came down, the stroller in front of him and the diaper bag on his back. By chance he stopped at a bench just a few yards from Slater.

Not looking at them, Slater could still watch in his peripheral vision. Harold lifted the kid out of the stroller and sat her on his lap, singing another song to her. "Nice Work If You Can Get It." Again not a kid song, but Harold had softened the edges for her. After he'd finished the last chorus, he spoke.

"Good god, little girl." His tone was gentle, incongruous with the content of his words. "Is it diaper time again? What is Mommie feeding you?"

It was dissonant to hear such tenderness from such a big guy, when his hard-core tats and his musculature implied he was a brawler. Slater watched as he wheeled the kid back up the path, and into the restroom, talking the whole time. Training the binoculars on the doorway, he saw Harold push the stroller out again a few minutes later. He paused to drop a white ball into the trash can. That had to be another dirty diaper. It didn't jibe with what Mary-Alice had said, that he never changed her.

As Harold pushed the stroller on the path, moving leisurely again, Slater rose and watched them through the glasses.

"Are you looking at girls?"

He dropped the binoculars and looked at the guy who'd spoken, standing nearby. Tall, with gray hair, he had a stupid grin on his face.

"I'm bird-watching, toots. Not that it's any of your business."

"The kind of birds that wear hot pants, I'm thinking."

"There's a species that's called spread out before I punch you in the face," Slater said. "Would you like to see that one up close?"

He scowled. "I'm just making conversation. You don't have to be a dick about it."

Slater walked away, and checked the time on his phone. He was attracting too much attention. Maybe he'd seen enough of Harold. He headed back to his car.

When he got behind the wheel, he checked Svetlana's software. The diaper-bag cameras had already recorded several hours of video. He sent Etta a text:

Do you have time to do some desk work this evening? Analyzing video.

Etta was an operative that he and Max used sometimes. Because the work was all new to her, she relished even the mundane tasks, like stakeouts and foot tails. And since she didn't work full-time in the cesspool like they did, she often came up with fresh perspectives and alternative explanations, and that had proven useful.

Nosing the Thunderbird out of the park, he drove through downtown to hilly Mount Washington, and pulled into Doris's driveway, and stopped behind her Buick.

Etta had responded to his text:

Sure! I'll come to the office.

He was about to text Doris, but then saw her step out the front door. Petite and graying, today she was wearing jeans and a stripey top. She climbed in the passenger side and leaned over to kiss him.

"My beautiful son."

Her brow furrowed, and she cupped his chin with her hand, and touched his mouth with her thumb.

Slater scowled. "Knock it off."

"What happened to your lip?"

"I nicked myself shaving."

"Don't lie to me."

Dropping the transmission into gear, Slater huffed and backed out of the driveway. "Someone didn't like the look of my face."

"You can't be fighting," she said intently.

"I know that." Cruising down the hill, he gestured to his phone in its dash mount. "Put your friend's address into my navigation app."

"No need," Doris said. "I know where she lives."

"You say that now, but then we'll be circling the neighborhood, looking for a bungalow with a red door, or is it a Tudor with a blue roof? Wait, did she move to Palm Springs?"

Doris waved at the windshield. "This is the southbound ramp. We're going the other way."

"Damn it," he snapped, and twisted his head to shoulder-check, then pulled back into the street. "Usually when I leave your place I'm headed back to civilization."

"In no way is my neighborhood uncivilized."

Slater laughed, turning onto the other ramp. "You know what I mean."

"I don't think I've heard you laugh since you were twelve years old. Despite your bruised lip, you're certainly in a good mood."

"I guess maybe I am."

"Is it your romantic narrative complex?" Doris said.

"It's all about Pike." He merged into the flow of the traffic on the parkway. "Things are evolving. We're getting more familiar. I still feel good with him, and we're both happy when we're together. Happy just to look at each other, and agreeing on everything."

"That's called the connected phase," she said. "Next comes the high phase."

"Good god, woman. You sound like a shrink."

"It's just pop psychology."

"You sent me to so many of them," Slater said. "I wouldn't be surprised if you got a psych degree by osmosis."

"They helped you, though. You're stable and healthy."

"I don't think that's true. I've been told more than once that I'm an emotional wreck."

"You're not that way when you're around me. I bet Pike wouldn't say that either."

Doris actually did know exactly where her friend's house was, on the backstreets of Pasadena, and they pulled up in front of it, a bungalow on a small lot. Doris climbed out and unlatched the gate, stepping into the yard. The lawn was patchy and brown.

"This must be the tree she was talking about,"

Slater said, looking it over. There was some shrubbery next to the house, but this was the only tree out front.

"It looks like she's not watering the grass," Doris said. "It's mostly dead."

"Her water agency probably told her she had to stop. Some of them are fining people with overly green turf."

A woman stepped out the front door of the house. About Doris's age, she was stout and had butched brown hair, wearing jeans and a billowy cotton blouse. They walked over to her.

"I'm Slater."

"Oh, we've met," she said. "A long time ago. At your father's funeral. My name is Daphne."

"Daphne was one of the water nymphs," Slater said. "She turned into a laurel tree."

"I can't believe you know that."

"There's lots of laurels in the genus *Daphne*."

"Don't underestimate my son," Doris said. "He's no dunce."

"I actually don't mind when people assume I'm stupid," he said. "It gives me an advantage in my work."

Doris raised her voice. "This isn't that kind of work."

"Didn't you used to be something of a ruffian?" Daphne said.

"I still am, but that's not incompatible with knowing who Daphne was." Slater waved a hand. "The boyfriend and I are reading Ovid. The story about Daphne stuck in my mind because it explains exactly why it's the scientific name for the laurels."

"Slater's not a ruffian," Doris said. "He never really was."

"As I remember it, though, there was always tsuris. He caused you a lot of heartache."

Slater winced. "Unfortunately that's also an on-going issue."

Doris wrapped an arm around his waist and squeezed. "And here he is today, with an associate degree in horticulture, in your front yard, expressly to help you out."

"That's the tree I'm having trouble with," Daphne said, gesturing to it.

"Use small words," Slater said, walking over to it, "so that I can understand."

She frowned as they followed him. "It was here when I bought the place. I think it's some kind of maple. It turns red in the fall."

"It's a *Liquidambar*," he said.

"I've been hosing it like crazy and it still looks dried out."

"Save your water—it won't help. This tree has other problems." He pulled a leaf off a branch. "It shouldn't have any leaves right now. It's so distressed it thinks it's still fall."

"That's true," Daphne said. "It's usually bare in winter."

Slater handed her the leaf. "This pattern of damage is called leaf scorch."

"From the heat?"

"It's a bacterial infection."

"Can I treat it?"

"You can, but I suspect there's no point. See this?" He pointed to the bark on the trunk and picked some off. "That's evidence of an insect called a shot hole borer. It can't be treated. Unfortunately it's terminal."

She frowned. "Why can't you treat it? There must be a spray."

"The borers reproduce inside the wood, so you can't get to them. In forests the way they manage infestations is to cut down the infected trees."

"So watering it won't help." Daphne's brow furrowed. "I thought the problem was about the drought."

"Big picture, it is about the drought. LA was never supposed to be wet enough for a tree like this."

"It's not local?" Doris said.

"It's native to the Southeast. People planted stuff like this in the boom times in the last century, but it's not supposed to be here. Susceptibility to disease and the diseases themselves are about being in the wrong climate."

Daphne folded her arms. "So what can I do?"

"Cut it down before it falls down. Replace it and the lawn and the shrubbery over there with native species. I can send you the names of some landscapers who do natives."

"It seems unfortunate," Doris said. "It's a big tree."

"You're not alone," Slater said. "It's happening everywhere. They're cutting down thousands of infected shade trees on public land. *Liquidambars* are street trees in some places, and those are gradually coming down too. In thirty years this town is going to look a lot more like Vegas or Phoenix. The era of the shady lush oasis is drawing to a close."

"That's not what I was hoping to hear," Daphne said.

"The upside is that whatever you spend on putting in natives, you'll save on your water bill. I bet your water agency has money for you to take out the lawn too."

Her eyes teared up, and she covered her mouth with a fist.

"Oh, sweetie," Doris said, and put an arm around her.

"It's sad to lose something so beautiful," Slater said. "But it's like a person when they're on their deathbed. You don't keep pushing food on them, or keep them alive with machines. When it's time you let them go with dignity."

She cleared her throat. "I get it, Slater."

"There are lots of California natives that explode with color all year round. Instead of a tree and some grass you can have dozens of species." He waved at the yard. "Take action soon, and a year from now the vibrant variety here will blow your mind."

SIX

WHEN HE AND DORIS got back into the Thunderbird, Slater spent a minute with his phone.

"I'm sending you contact info for a landscaper who can help her," he said, "so I won't forget."

Eventually he started the engine and pulled into the street.

"She was rude to you," Doris said, "and you were still really compassionate with her."

"You think? Most people are rude to me most of the time. I don't know her, so I don't care what she thinks of me. I did have to give her some very bad news."

"But you didn't say, 'Snap out of it. It's just a tree.'"

"That tree is older than all of us. It's seen more sunrises than most people on this earth ever will. It's a tragic loss."

"It was hard for her. I guess bad news always is."

"The truth is better than not knowing, don't you

think?" he said. "Even when it's painful, the truth is the golden thread that ties the world together."

She reached over and squeezed his arm. "My son, the philosopher."

When they pulled into Doris's driveway, he leaned over to kiss her. "Love you."

He watched her climb out, then backed into the street, and cruised downtown to his office.

Etta was already here, sitting at the front desk. Curvy and with short black hair, she'd been working more for Max recently, but she'd learned a lot about the trade from both of them. Her main gig was teaching middle school. It had to be a cushy gig, Slater had decided, because she seemed to have plenty of free time away from it.

"How's that long drink of water?" Etta said.

"Pike?" Slater put his hands on his hips. "He's in Albuquerque. He says the bloom is off the rose."

She winced. "Ouch."

"Do you think that means he's getting sick of me?"

"If he was sick of you, he wouldn't show up. It just means he's getting familiar with you. He's seeing you for who you are. All of you—all your assets, all your flaws."

Slater frowned. "It's not like that's a one-way street. He's got plenty of those too."

"It sounds like you still want him around, though."

"The dick wants what the dick wants. I can't keep my hands off him."

"I know it's more than that," Etta said. "You called your relationship a narrative complex, and I heard the *l* word mentioned. That's beyond sex."

Slater waved a hand. "I can't stop thinking about the guy. I want him to feel happy. I want to iron his shirts for him. I don't even know how to do that. Is that love?"

"Sounds like it to me," she said, and chuckled. "So what's on the video?"

"If the cameras held up, it should be a guy with his kid," Slater said. "I figured you work with kids, so you can tell me what kind of parent he is."

He wheeled his chair out of his office, and sat next to her, and explained how he'd set up surveillance on Harold and the kid. Grabbing the mouse, he clicked around to connect to Svetlana's video storage server.

"How old is the child?" Etta said.

"I think it's a yearling," he said, peering at the screen.

"That's how you talk about horses. People are he, she, or they. And aim for a phrase like 'one year old.'"

"You're such a teacher." Slater glanced at her sidelong. "I concede that she's *Homo sapiens*. Age eleven months. Her name is Rose."

"Aw. That's sweet."

"Are you going to reproduce?" he said, still clicking at the screen. "You have the equipment for it."

"I deal with mouthy tweens all day. Why would I bring one into my life full-time?"

The video came up as side-by-side images, one for each camera in the diaper bag, with a lone audio feed. Slater fast-forwarded through the first part, where both screens were dark, and let it play when the first images appeared. Both frames showed vague shapes and light whirling around, then suddenly stopped.

One camera went dark, and the other showed the framing of an unfinished wall in the distance—inside Mary-Alice's industrial apartment. No one was in view, but there were voices, and the audio was clear.

"How's my little girl? I've missed you." It was Harold, speaking in a gentle singsong voice.

"You have to bring her back on time." Mary-Alice's voice was much louder. "You're always late."

"I was late once," Harold said, still using a gentle tone. "And don't harsh me in front of Rose."

Etta reached for the keyboard to pause the playback. "She knows she's being taped. She's saying that to get it into the record."

"I think you're probably right."

She frowned. "I thought we weren't supposed to tell the clients about recording devices. Plausible deniability."

"I didn't have much choice," Slater said. "I needed to get the cameras into the diaper bag. Mary-Alice was in charge of the bag. She doesn't actually know it's cameras. She probably thinks it's just a mike."

He fast-forwarded through most of the morning's park visit, as he'd been there in person, but paused occasionally to listen to Harold. He was talking non-stop, and sometimes singing, mostly familiar pop songs.

At one point, when Harold had the kid standing in his lap, Slater clicked to watch it at normal speed. One of the video frames showed the pair of them in profile, and the other showed an empty stretch of park bench. He must have set the bag beside him.

"Who loves Rose?" Harold said, bouncing her up and down, his big hands wrapped around her. "Who's

Daddy's special little girlfriend?"

"You can't date a baby," Slater muttered. "Straight people are crazy."

Etta shifted in her chair. "Preach."

"I think we should go look at the turtles," Harold said. "Does Rose want to go look at the turtles? They're in the Japanese garden, but I don't think they're Japanese turtles."

Clicking the mouse, Slater sped through more of it, the walk up to the turtle pond, and the diaper change in the restroom, and strolling. Later on, the cameras stopped on a dim static image of worn carpet.

"That must be the floor of the pickup," Slater said.

Sure enough, when he let it play for a moment, there was engine noise, with Harold's voice over it. He was singing "Let It Be," Slater realized.

"Dude can actually carry a tune," Etta said.

Slater scoffed and fast-forwarded. After more jumbled video, the image stopped again. It was a room with kitchen cupboards in one frame and a bright window in the other. Below the window was a gray expanse. The top of a table.

Harold's shirt appeared, with his belt and his thick forearms, and he spread a blanket on the table, then set the kid on it. The camera was so close that it only showed the kid's arm and torso as she babbled and wiggled around. Listening to the audio, Harold was singing a song about diapers—he was changing her.

Eventually he picked her up again and stepped out of frame. They could still hear him talking non-stop. Slater fast-forwarded through some of it, but each time he let it play, Harold was either singing or talking, mostly spouting inanities and saying things the kid was too young to answer to: "Is Rose feeling a little warm? Should we take off your sweater?" At one point he recited a rhyming story about a giraffe.

"He's reading from a book," Etta said.

Later Harold stepped back into the video frame and set the kid on the table again.

"Didn't he just change her diaper?" Slater demanded.

"We've been fast-forwarding. From the time stamp that was over an hour ago."

"Still, how often do you need to do that?"

"It depends," Etta said, gazing at the screen. "It happens that way sometimes, where they need a change every few hours."

He fast-forwarded some more, until the video jumbled around again. They were in the Tacoma, with Harold singing all the way, and then in Mary-Alice's place. One camera showed the oversize sink, and the other Mary-Alice's shirt.

"She smells terrible," Mary-Alice said, her tone loud and jarring. "You didn't change her."

"What are you talking about? I went through a whole package of diapers today. She smells like springtime in the park right now."

After Harold left, Mary-Alice lifted the bag, and put it in a cupboard, and both cameras went black.

"She knows about the surveillance," Etta said, "and she doesn't want to be recorded."

Slater rubbed his eyes. "All the yapping, all the singing. The guy seems brain damaged."

"It actually means he's a good parent. The science says that talking to them is the best way to help them develop language skills. What you say to them doesn't matter that much, but the talking itself is huge. The more you talk to them, the quicker they learn, and the more verbal they become. Language skills are the key to so many other things. He's actively inducing intelligence in her."

"Did you see any evidence that he was abusive?"

"There's not even a whiff of that." She waved a hand. "If every parent was like him, we wouldn't need social workers anymore. Did your client say she saw him being abusive?"

"It doesn't wash, does it."

"If she told you he was harming the kid, I'd say she's lying to you."

Slater nodded. "What do I owe you?"

"You don't have to pay me for sitting here on my butt and gossiping."

"You worked on my case, and you gave me your actionable professional insights. I have to pay you. Besides, it's Saturday night. I bet Safiya is furious that you're not at home munching her carpet."

"Nice," she said flatly, and frowned. "Just for that, give me a hundo."

"Done."

He stood up to pull out his wad of cash, and peeled off a C-note, and handed it over. Once he'd rolled his chair back into his office, he locked up, and they rode down in the elevator together. It was dark out—they'd been watching those blear-inducing videos for longer than he thought.

Etta waved good-bye and climbed into her little red Prius, and Slater got into the Thunderbird, and drove to his house. Upstairs he poured his ration and stretched out on the sofa with the tumbler. There was good house music on Saturday night, and he turned on the radio.

Normally this was the time of day he'd sniff around for a hookup, before he started drinking, but he wanted to see what it was like not to do that, what it might feel like to commit to fucking only the one guy. Weird, he realized. It just felt weird. He slurped at the heady golden elixir and sank into the music.

A while later his phone buzzed, and he lifted it off the floor. The caller ID said REDDY KILOWATT. His nickname for Pike. He turned down the radio.

"It's the man with a million volts in his pants," Slater said as he picked up.

"It's nice to hear your voice," Pike said, and they chatted for a while, catching up on the details of the day.

"Do you want to read to me?" Slater said.

"I don't know. I'm kind of wiped out."

"You took the book. I need to know what happens to Aeneas on that damn boat." He wasn't concerned about Aeneas, not really. It was just so he could hear Pike's voice.

"I guess if I'm talking to you, I know you're not out fucking someone else."

"I deserved that."

"Five minutes," Pike said. "Then I have to crash. It's later here."

"Is that how time zones work?"

"Thin ice, forty-niner," he said, and chuckled.

He heard pages riffling, and then Pike spoke.

"Here it is: 'As Aeneas and the sibyl approached the riverbank, Charon told them to stop. I don't ferry the living, he said. Only the dead …'"

SEVEN

IN THE MORNING SLATER's head felt clear. That meant he hadn't overdone it with the bourbon. Maybe just talking to Pike was making him into a better man. He cast off the covers and went upstairs to make coffee. There was an incidentally vegan Pop-Tart in the pantry cupboard, and he ripped off the wrapper, and carried it and a steaming mug of java out to the deck. It was cold out but the bright sunlight felt good.

Checking his tracking software, he saw that Harold's ride was at his place on Gage. It made sense that the repair shop wouldn't be working on Sunday. At this point Slater knew enough about this guy that he could probably wrap up the investigation. But the twelve-step meeting still nagged at him. Just because Harold was going to meetings didn't mean he wasn't a drunk, or a doper, or a dealer. He'd learn more if he sat on his house for a while. Dealers had lots of visitors, especially on weekends.

Once he was dressed he went down to the garage and cruised to Harold's neighborhood. The red Tacoma was here, parked in front of Harold's place. There was an open street space across from his building, and Slater pulled in, and rolled down his window, and grabbed his binoculars. It looked to be one of those 1950s four-up, four-down jobs—eight apartments on two floors with exterior stairs. There were so many of those all over the metropolis. He didn't even know which unit was Harold's—his pad might be farther back. But he had a good view of the walkway onto the property, the way in for anyone coming or going, and that was his focus now, the foot traffic. The binoculars brought him up close, but it also limited his field of view—he never saw it coming.

The glasses went dark, and he dropped them to find Harold looming there, standing in the street next to his car, his face contorted with anger. Before Slater could say anything, Harold leaned in and punched him through the open window.

His head snapped sideways, and he instinctively leaned away. There was no way to fight back—Harold was in control of the car door. He touched his nose. It felt numb. It was bleeding, he realized.

"Damn it," Slater snapped. "Was that really necessary?"

"Tell Wilma I don't know anything," Harold shouted. "I've never known anything."

"The fuck is Wilma?" Slater wiped at his upper lip, and saw his fingers come away covered in blood. "That was kind of a dick move when you know I can't punch back."

Harold took a step along the Thunderbird's fender

and flashed his palms. "Get out of the car, then. Go ahead—come at me."

"We both know that would be suicide."

"Why are you following me?" he demanded. "Why not just knock on my door and ask me about Lance?"

"I don't know who that is," Slater said, keeping his voice as calm as he could. "I'm going to drive away now, so I can go put some ice on this mess."

"You can't drive like that." Harold reached for the handle and pulled the door open a few inches. "I have ice. Come upstairs."

Slater eyed him. "Seriously?"

"I feel a little bad," he said. "I hope it's not broken."

"I don't think it is." He pulled his keys out of the ignition and stepped out. "You'd better not be planning to take another poke at me."

His ears were ringing and he felt a little dazed as he followed Harold across to the opposite sidewalk, and up the stairs, and into his apartment. It was the closest one to the street, and the living room window looked out at Gage—he'd probably spotted Slater from here, and gone out the back way so that he could sneak up on him.

Harold reached into the bathroom and flipped on the light, and Slater stepped in and studied his reflection in the mirror. It looked worse than it probably was, the bright red on his lip, all the lurid red streaks on his chin and his neck. The bleeding seemed to have stopped already. In the sink he washed the blood off his face and his hands.

As he stepped back into the kitchen, Harold pulled open the freezer and handed him a packet of peas. He sat at the kitchen table, familiar from the video as the one where he'd changed the kid yesterday, and folded his massive arms.

Dropping into the chair across from him, Slater pressed the peas onto his face and groaned. The cold felt good, as it soothed the throbbing, and took the edge off the dull ache that was setting in.

"It's been a minute since Wilma sent anyone," Harold said. "What's changed with her?"

Slater shifted the packet of peas to peer at him with one eye. "I don't know who that is."

"Don't lie to me. I saw your ride at my shop, bruh. Then Tom down the block calls me about a shady-looking Mexican driving an old T-bird. Today I see the same car in front of my house."

"I'm not Mexican," Slater said, and scowled. "Is Tom the guy with the Chihuahua?"

"You've met."

"He busted my chops for just walking past him."

"That makes him a good neighbor. He's also so old that he could ID your wheels. He said his pops drove one of those when they were new."

"I guess I'm not as stealthy as I think I am."

"Or you need to drive a less unique car. There's probably three of those on the road in the whole damn city." Harold threw up a hand. "So why are you following me?"

"I can't really discuss my work."

"So it is Wilma." He frowned. "Maybe I really should break your nose."

"You don't have the element of surprise anymore. I'd be able to inflict a little pain too."

Harold sighed. "I don't want to be a dick. Really,

I don't. But sometimes life requires it."

"I get it. You're a big dude. I'm sure people expect you to use force."

"It's a stereotype. But I do know how to handle myself."

Slater could feel his eyes on him, see them burning with curiosity. The number-one rule in his business was that his loyalty had to be with his client, regardless of whether they lied to him, or whether he got a better offer. But he knew how frustrated the guy must be, and he knew Harold wasn't abusing his kid.

"Here's the thing," Slater said. "You're in a custody dispute right now."

"I'm not. That's been sorted out. The court says I get two days a week and holidays. Bam, judge's orders." He sat back, and furrowed his brow, and spoke in a softer tone. "I know I've got problems. I've done some things."

"Whatever you've done, it doesn't mean you're unfit to be a father. Nobody's beyond redemption. You're working on it, right?"

"I'm in program, if that's what you mean. I've been dry for almost three years. Those little anniversary chips are the most valuable pieces of jewelry I own."

"I know getting sober is damn hard work."

"I'm not going to believe that you work for the county," Harold said. "Those people wear their ID on a lanyard and look like doughnut-eating desk jockeys. That's not you."

"I don't work for the county."

"That means you're private. So it's Mary-Alice." He scoffed. "I know what she's doing."

"What is she doing?"

"Trying to reopen the custody thing." He raised his voice. "It's been settled. Why would she put me through that again? And how long have you been on my ass? What are you going to tell her?"

"There's nothing to tell her," Slater said. "You're actually a pretty dull guy."

"Will you whine to her about today? 'Oh, poor me, Harold punched me in the face.'"

"That has nothing to do with Mary-Alice, or your kid." He shrugged. "I would have done the same thing."

Harold watched him for a moment. "OK," he said finally.

"So who's Wilma? Another angry ex?"

He chuckled. "I wouldn't sleep with her on a bet. But she's angry, all right."

"She sends guys like me after you?" Slater shifted the peas to the other side of his face.

"Not lately. She was my Uncle Lance's business partner. He's been missing for a while. She thinks I might know where he is."

"I bet there's money involved."

"Oh, yeah. Stupid piles of it. They were in the funny money business. Cryptocurrency."

Slater rose and rinsed the bag of peas in the kitchen sink.

"Thanks for this," he said, and tossed it in the freezer.

"You're not going to make trouble for me?"

"I'm getting paid to find out how you treat your kid. I'm not going to lie about it."

"How would you know anything about that?"

"I saw you in the park yesterday," Slater said. "I

know you're a good father."

Harold sighed. "Well, you can tell my old lady to go fuck herself."

"I might not use those exact words, but I'll put that in the subtext."

He walked out and trotted down the stairs to the sidewalk. What a freaking idiot he was for getting made. Spotted from half a block away and punched in the face like a damn tyro. Pausing at the Tacoma, he stepped into the street and reached up into the wheel well to pull off the tracker, not even bothering to scan for potential eyewitnesses. He wasn't going to be surveilling Harold anymore, and these things weren't cheap.

Andy did hacking-type work for him sometimes, although he refused to call it that, claiming that he did "deep research." He'd be able to dig up the details a lot faster than Slater could.

Once he was behind the wheel of the Thunderbird, he texted Andy:

Are you home? I'll drop by.

His reply came before he'd even fired up the engine:

You can't.

Slater dialed his number, breathing hard as he listened to it ring.

When he picked up, Slater demanded, "What do you mean, I can't?"

"I mean you can't … come over," Andy said. "Is it work? Just tell me … on the phone, or email me the details."

"Are you still pissed that I'm getting sticky with Pike? I thought we were through that. I can't help how I feel."

"The world doesn't … revolve around you, Slater."

"Is that gunsel Kyle there to suck your cock? Careful not to muss his coiffure. One hair out of place and he'll storm out in tears."

"Tell me what you need," Andy said, "or I'm … hanging up."

Slater huffed. "I need you to look up a court case. I'll text you the names."

He ended the call and spent a minute thumb-typing the details, then took a breath. His nose was throbbing now, that persistent dull ache that he knew wouldn't go away any time soon. Pulling down the rearview mirror, he could see that it was definitely swollen.

"Idiot," he muttered. In the glove box he scrabbled for the bottle of ibuprofen, and shook a couple into his mouth.

Firing up the engine, he pulled into the street and drove to his office. The parking lot was empty, the lobby quiet, the factories abandoned on Sunday. Max wasn't here either, and he flicked on the lights as he stepped in.

Swinging his feet up onto his desk, he gazed at the statue of Pollux. The front-office likeness of Rey Pascual was probably enough tchotchkes for their little office suite, but Pollux had been a gift from Pike. He'd sent it before they'd even gotten together. Naked and standing with a horse, the little guy had great hair. Its twin, the plaster image of Castor, sat on Pike's desk.

Several news items popped up when he searched for "Lance" and "cryptocurrency." One of them bore the headline "Crypto Guru Lance Wiley Missing." This had to be the guy.

Scrolling down, Slater paused to study Lance's face in the photo that was buried in the article, a posed and styled corporate headshot, the guy looking at the camera with a confident smile. In his fifties, maybe, Lance had short gray hair, and even with the photo retouching, the lines on his face made it look like he spent a lot of time in the sun.

Reading another article from a traditional news site, he got a sense of what had happened with Lance. He'd created a crypto product with his partner, the woman that Harold had mentioned, Wilma. The thing had quickly shot up in value, attracting a lot of investment. That was hard to do, the writer said, as there were a hundred thousand distinct crypto products on the market, lots of them worth nothing, and lots of them straight-up scams, not even based on blockchain. Lance and Wilma's was deemed legit, but soon after the huge inflation in the value of their product, just before the big crypto crash, Lance had disappeared, along with a big chunk of the company's assets.

Sitting back, Slater rubbed his eyes. A hundred thousand different crypto products. All those freaking grifters. It seemed insane. Like the turtles crowding the pond where Lance had taken his kid, or the endless tents lining the streets of Skid Row.

Another article mentioned a bounty on Lance, with a mock wanted poster that bore the same corporate portrait photo of the guy with gray prison bars superimposed, emblazoned top and bottom with the words REWARD and $1 MILLION.

Odd that it didn't mention what agency had issued the bounty. Usually it was the feds—the FBI or the marshals. Digging deeper for details, he soon realized it wasn't really a bounty, just a private reward for information from a company—the company he'd founded with Wilma. Calling it a bounty implied some kind of legal proceeding, charges or an indictment or somebody jumping bail, but this was just sloppy pseudojournalism. Nothing else implied that Lance had ever been charged with anything.

Sitting back, Slater closed his eyes and focused on the throbbing pain in his nose. It was radiating across his face now. It was probably going to bruise. Why had he let himself get made like that? He was getting sloppy. In his pants his phone buzzed, and he pulled it out to check. A message from Andy:

Found your court case. Check your email.

When he pulled it up, he found a lengthy legal document, and sat up to peer at the screen. The names were right: Harold and Mary-Alice and Rose. The language was so dry, the text so boring, but there was no other way. He had to read through it.

The judgment was what Harold had told him— split custody, with two days for him and five for her. There was testimony and a couple of statements from three different social workers about Harold, confirming that he was attentive to the kid and competent as a parent. He had the right kind of car seat in his rig, they explained, and knew how to feed the kid, and he knew how to change a diaper. Slater had seen copious evidence of that himself.

He closed his eyes and massaged his temples. It all fit with what he'd seen. Harold hadn't lied to him, but Mary-Alice definitely had. Steeling himself, he swung his boots up onto his desk again and pulled his keyboard into his lap. It took a while to write the report for Mary-Alice, even though it wound up being less than three pages. As she'd requested he put it on their office letterhead.

When he was done with that, he pulled up the blank invoice they used, and thought about what to charge her. It had taken him a few days' effort. But this had been a penny-ante job from the get-go. Mary-Alice had lied to him, but then everybody lied to him, all the time—it was the default. He couldn't tax her just for doing that. He knew she wasn't wealthy, and based on what he'd seen, her diaper bill alone must be astronomical.

On the invoice he entered "$600," and at the bottom added "Paid in full," then attached it to an email, along with the report, and set it to send tomorrow. If she was going to bug him about it, he could put it off for another day, when his face wasn't throbbing.

Digging through the trial record again, he found the names of the child services staffers who'd spoken at the hearing. It was easy to track down their county email addresses, and he composed a note to them explaining that he'd been hired to observe Harold with Rose, and after many hours of observation, his assessment was that he was a competent and caring parent. He cited the examples of all the talking and singing and the diaper changes.

He didn't have to do that, stick his nose so far into

it, but Harold loved that baby fiercely. Why would he let Mary-Alice mess that up?

When he got back to his house, he went upstairs and pulled the bourbon out of the cupboard. It wasn't that late, and normally this is when he'd arrange a hookup, but getting a little tight right away would prevent that. He'd never risk letting a stranger into his house when he was impaired.

Pouring his ration into a tumbler, he added a little extra, to numb the pain and distract him from the embarrassment of getting punched in the face.

"Idiot," he muttered, thinking about it, and carried his glass over to the French doors. As he looked out at the city he took that first satisfying sip, relishing the burn and the fumes in his nose.

It felt bogus, not being able to fuck other people when he wanted to. Like an itch that he couldn't reach. Pike hadn't said he wanted exclusivity, not yet, but it felt like that was coming. Hobbled, he'd said. He'd feel hobbled. People did that to horses so they couldn't walk away, but it was an unnecessary cruelty, and it made them miserable. Was Slater really going to be able to put up with that?

EIGHT

WHEN SLATER WOKE, HE had a dreamy idea floating in his mind: a million clams. Imagine what he could do with that kind of scratch. Where had that come from?

As he swam up into consciousness, the memory flooded in: the reward for Lance. How could he not take a bite at that? He already had an inside contact. Work had been slow, and he'd let Mary-Alice off cheap. He needed to be doing something to generate revenue.

Sitting up, he realized his nose still hurt, the dull throb ramping up as his body started to move. In the bathroom mirror it definitely looked a little swollen. But at least it hadn't bruised.

Once he'd made coffee, he sat out on the deck to sip it, shivering in the chill morning air. He thought through how to approach the Lance thing. It was Monday—Harold would be at work.

After he'd dressed, he went down to his garage,

and backed the Thunderbird into the street, then headed south to Murdertown. Pulling up at the repair shop, he walked into one of the open bays. Harold was here, wearing his blue coveralls, standing under the front end of the vehicle on the lift. When he glanced up, he frowned in recognition and stepped out from under the car.

"You again. How's your nose?"

"I'll survive," Slater said. "So I've been reading about Lance. Is he missing by choice? Did he get kidnapped? Do you think someone could have croaked him?"

"Why are you interested in Lance?"

"His former business partner put out a reward for information on him."

Harold scoffed. "Wilma. That woman is trouble. If you want my advice, steer clear of her. Forget you ever heard that name."

"Do you think she iced him?"

"She thinks he's alive too, or there wouldn't be a reward."

"That might just be a cover story," Slater said.

"Well, she wouldn't be harassing me if she knew he was dead. If Wilma had croaked him, she'd want me and everybody else to forget all about him."

"So you think Lance is alive. Has he been in contact?"

"He didn't tell me anything before he left," Harold said, absently rubbing his grease-blackened knuckles with his palm. "I know him. He's smart. If he doesn't want to be found, you're not going to find him."

"What kind of person is he?"

"Like I said, smart. Decent. A little eccentric

sometimes. I think that helped him come up with that funny-money idea. His alternative way of thinking."

Slater nodded. "He and Wilma made a lot of lettuce out of thin air."

"Lance did the computer part of it," Harold said. "The coding. I'm not even sure how Wilma got involved."

"Did you spend time with her before Lance disappeared, or in the office?"

"I wasn't really paying attention to him or to Wilma when they were building the company. I had other priorities. I know Lance got stupid rich in a big hurry. Before he left he gave me some money for Rose's future."

"So why are you still working?"

"It's for Rose, not for me. It's not enough to retire on anyway. Just enough to supplement her expenses and the child support I have to pay Mary-Alice. I put most of it in a college fund." His eyes narrowed. "My ex doesn't know anything about that. Let's keep it that way."

He waved dismissively. "I'm all done with her. Does Lance have other family?"

"Not close relations," Harold said. "He never got married. I guess he couldn't have, until recently. I think he's one of your people."

Slater put his hands on his hips. "My people? You mean hot, and smart, and charming?"

"I mean he's a man's man. He never told me that, but it's not hard to connect the dots."

"How did you peg me as gay?"

"Straight guys don't usually check out my crotch."

"To be fair," Slater said, raising his eyebrows,

"even in those coveralls, it does appear that you're stacked."

"You know, I've been told the way to be charming with women is not to comment on their appearance."

"You're no woman, big guy."

"And you're never going to know for sure what's in my pants."

Slater chuckled and walked back to his car.

One of the articles he'd read about the crypto product that Lance and Wilma had created also mentioned their office space. Once he was behind the wheel, he spent a minute with his phone, and eventually found it again. The office was in WeHo, and a map search showed that it was still in the same place, right on the edge of Boystown. He plugged the address into his navigation and pulled into the traffic.

He remembered this building, he realized, as he drove up on it. Low-slung and dark-shingled, it had a fuggly 1970s vibe. It used to be a talent agency, with a stupid tickertape sign along the eaves, and before that it had been a menswear store. Up the block he found an open meter, and fed it quarters, and walked back toward the place.

When he stepped inside, a uniformed guard loomed near the entrance. Beefy and dark, he looked Samoan, maybe, like Etta, and he wore a sidearm on his hip. It seemed odd that a small office would have armed security. Stepping into his path, the guy met his gaze.

"Deliveries are around back."

"I'm not the post office, toots," Slater said, and stepped around him.

The guard extended an arm to block his way, and

Slater turned to slap him, left and then right, a firm kovac. The guard planted a palm on his chest and shoved hard, sending Slater stumbling back a few steps.

"Why would you do that when you know I'm armed?" the guy demanded, his face contorted with anger.

"Are you seriously going to draw down on me?"

From the desk farther inside a woman in a pale-blue suit rose and shouted at them. "Stop it."

Slater eyed her as she stepped over. "You hired this gorilla to give static to everyone who walks through the door?"

The guard jutted his flabby chin. "Only the trash."

Slater moved toward him, but the woman quickly stepped in front of him.

"Calm down," she demanded.

It was impressive that she'd get between them—this woman was no stranger to dustups.

She turned and eyed the guard. "Gene, catch yourself. Why don't you step outside for a minute?"

His eyes went dead, and without a word, he walked toward the entrance.

"You've got him on a short leash," Slater said.

"Why did you do that?" she demanded.

"I didn't do anything. It's called self-defense."

She stepped back to her desk, the only one in the lobby, but didn't sit down. Thin, with her tight afro in delicate twists, she looked to be around thirty. As he followed her over, Slater saw the name plate on her desk: DESIREE. Besides a laptop and a lamp the only other thing on the desktop was a plastic card. He knew that lurid purple logo—it was for a gym chain. That place was expensive. Maybe these people really did have more money than they knew what to do with.

"There's a process for investors," Desiree said. "It's outlined in the material we sent. You can't just show up here."

"Do I look like an investor?" Slater demanded.

"So what is this regarding?"

"Information on the whereabouts of Lance Wiley."

Her brow furrowed, and she studied his face. "Can you wait here for a moment?" She stepped away, but then turned back. "Do you have a card?"

Slater dug a business card out of his hip pocket and handed it to her, and she studied it as she walked into the back. He glanced around the lobby while he waited. Big windows looked out on the traffic of the boulevard, and the carpet had a colorful pattern in it. Unlike her gym membership, the vibe here wasn't especially pretentious. The place actually looked a little run-down—the carpet was worn around the entrance, and one of the glass light fixtures overhead had a visible crack in it.

Desiree returned a moment later and gestured for him to follow her. Farther back they stepped into a big office, with floor-to-ceiling windows onto a lush green courtyard. That had to be illegal, watering the landscape so much, babying all those piggy tropical plants. But surrounded by the building, the little yard was hidden from the view of anyone who could spank them for it.

As he walked in, Desiree stepped back out and closed the door, and the woman behind the desk rose.

This had to be Wilma. In her forties, at least, she didn't look surgeried, not yet. Maybe some lip filler. Her dark Latin hair was swept back, and she wore an embroidered vest and dark trousers.

"Mr. Ibáñez," she said.

"It's just Slater." He gestured to the bookshelf along the wall behind her. In the middle was a gold statue, given pride of place with lots of air around it, lit from above by a spotlight. "Is that an Emmy?"

Wilma spoke in a weird creaky voice. "Let's go for a walk."

His eyes narrowed. "No thanks."

"You don't remember *Wilma's Walks*? I earned that Emmy when I was twelve. My character opened every episode with that line." She repeated it, with the same unsettling intonation: "Let's go for a walk."

"I guess I'm too old for that series."

"You flatter me. More like it's too old for you. That's why I tell people to call me Wilma. For many years I was Wilma on the small screen."

"What was your name before that?"

She grinned. "Methanie. Short form Meth. The funny part is that my parents never took drugs."

Slater nodded. "Yeah, I would have changed it too."

"Sit down," she said, and gestured to the chair in front of her big glass-topped desk. Once she was seated, Wilma folded her arms on the blotter and met his gaze. "Your card says you're an insurance investigator. Are you also a bounty hunter?"

"Bounty hunters don't go after private rewards."

"But you want the money."

"Tell me about that."

Wilma chuckled. "I really want to track down Lance. I can pay you a million dollars if you bring him to me."

"That seems a bit Wild West," Slater said. "Will you pay me if I can tell you where to find him? Unless he's charged with something, I can't make him do anything."

"He ripped me off, Slater." She held his gaze, and spoke intently. "Lance stole over a billion dollars from the company."

"Billion, with a *b*?" He frowned. "In cash?"

"In coin."

That wasn't at all the same as money, he knew. But he didn't say that. "You built the crypto thing together, correct?"

Wilma scowled. "He sold up and disappeared."

"But he didn't sell everything, or you wouldn't be here."

"He left me way overexposed. I was barely able to survive, and now I have to deal with all the investors on my own."

"Did anyone report him missing to the police?"

She sat back. "I tried, but they said there was evidence he'd left town of his own accord. By their standards they couldn't see any crime."

"What evidence did they cite?" Slater said.

"He was living in one of those long-term hotels." She waved a hand. "The cops said he checked out right before he went missing. I went to the hotel myself. One of the staff told me he'd helped Lance load all his stuff into his car. The guy asked him where he was headed, with all his worldly possessions, and Lance just told him he needed a fresh start."

"What was he driving?"

Wilma shook her head. "I tried that already. He sold his car the same day. Before he even got out of LA. There's no record of a subsequent vehicle registered to him. Maybe someone helped him, and bought a car in their name, or maybe he stole one. Pulling that thread didn't lead anywhere."

"Do you have any idea where he might have been headed when he disappeared?"

"He just stopped showing up for work. That's when I realized the money was gone."

"Did he say good-bye to anyone, or leave a note?"

"Nothing like that."

"What kind of guy was he?" Slater said.

"It's hard to be objective. I've been angry with him for a very long time. But I'd say he was smart." She raised her eyebrows. "So what leads do you have so far?"

"I'm really just getting started."

She looked away. "I'd hoped maybe you'd made some progress already. I won't discourage you from trying, although lots of others have. You know it'll be worth your while."

Slater rose and walked out to the lobby. Desiree wasn't at her desk, but the security guard was back. He fixed Slater with a cold glare as he walked out.

Once he was behind the wheel of the Thunderbird, he pulled out his phone. There was a voicemail from Mary-Alice, but he was done with her, and he deleted it without listening to it. When he checked on Pike's flight, he saw that his plane was actually landing a few minutes early. He needed to get to LAX.

Pulling into the traffic, Slater was soon crawling along in front of the terminal, eyeing the legion of weary pedestrians crowding the curb. Pike waved at him from up ahead, and flashed that smile. Such a beautiful man. His heart pounded at the sight of him. Slater pulled ahead and nosed in to the curb.

Pike was wearing his civvies today instead of his office drag. They were both getting better at navigating the commute—he knew Pike had gone directly to the airport from work, so he must have taken a change of clothes.

Heaving his bag into the backseat, Pike climbed in, and leaned over to kiss him, exploring his mouth, lingering in it. Eventually he pulled back and furrowed his brow.

"What happened to your nose?"

"I got too close to a target," Slater said. "Does it look bad?"

"Just a little swollen. At least it's not broken. Do you need me to go give him a tune-up?"

Slater scoffed and pulled away from the curb, eyeing the traffic in his side mirror. "We have a stop to make before we go to my place."

"I'm in no rush to get anywhere. Is it work, or an errand? Please tell me you don't need any more furniture. Schlepping around those stores is a serious grind."

Slater chuckled. "I want you to meet someone."

As he merged onto the freeway, he told Pike about getting punched in the face, and about Harold, and the kid. The navigation took him east to the 710. That felt like overshooting East LA, but the traffic wasn't too heavy, and soon they rolled into the cemetery. Slater found the right section, and parked, and they both climbed out. He led the way across the turf, mostly dead and yellow now, with a few patches of winter weeds. He stopped at the headstone marked IBANEZ.

"My old man," Slater said.

Pike squeezed him around the waist. "I'm so sorry he left you."

"It took me a long time to forgive him for that. To accept that it wasn't his choice."

"Do you come by here often?"

"Once in a while. I sit here and fill him in on my train wreck of a life."

Pike chuckled. "I bet he'd be proud of you."

"Pop, this is Pike," Slater said, eyeing the headstone. "He can be a bit of a hard-ass. The day we met he actually had the nerve to tase me. But I'm madly in love with him anyway."

———·———

AT SLATER'S HOUSE PIKE carried his suitcase up to the bedroom.

"Maybe we can eat out," Slater said.

"That place that's in an old theater? I loved the cauliflower wings."

It was on Sunset, close enough to walk, and as they headed out, Slater twisted his key to bolt the front door. Farther down the block Pike pointed to a street tree as they strode past.

"In a city that doesn't have winter, why would you plant something that loses its leaves?"

"We have winter," Slater said. "It's freezing cold right now."

He chuckled. "I don't even need a jacket."

"That's a jacaranda. In a few months it's going to be a cloud of purple haze. It blossoms a lot before it leafs out."

"Nice."

"It depends on your perspective," Slater said. "The blossoms drop and make a mess of the streets, and they smell like dick cheese. This guy in the newspaper says jacarandas are all flash, no substance."

"Then it sounds like it's right at home in this burg. A fitting symbol for the city of angels. One of the people in my office asked me, 'What do you do when you're out there? Float around with the rest of the airheads?'"

"I'm not an airhead," Slater said, and shot him a look. "But in a way that rings true. About the tree being symbolic. Like most Angelenos its origins are on the other side of the planet. Brazil, maybe, or South Africa."

"I've never seen you read the newspaper," Pike said.

"Doris does. Then she forwards me the highlights. Mostly stories about gardening and political corruption."

After they'd eaten, sated and lounging at the table in the restaurant, Pike moved his plate aside and met his eye.

"Truth time."

Slater groaned and shifted in his chair. "Do I need to have a drink first?"

"It's about the sex stuff. I know that exclusivity is square."

"I don't care about that. It's more that I'm just not used to it."

"You know I'm in a rules-based job," Pike said, "and you've got your booze rules. Maybe we can add some general rules to our narrative complex."

"In your work the rules are pretty black-and-white. No guns on airplanes, and you can't have more than ten pounds of black powder."

"In California it's five pounds, but you're on the right track."

Slater waved a hand. "What kind of rules?"

"You don't fuck other people when I'm in town."

"Agreed. That's easy."

"Unless it's a three-way," Pike said, raising his eyebrows, "and we're both there. That was pretty damn hot."

"We'll keep that option open."

"You only do it for work or for stress release, not as a fun adventure type deal."

He nodded. "That's totally reasonable."

"The emotional part has to be more restrictive. It's about sex only. You can't romance anyone else. Only me."

"There is no one else," Slater said. "I can't even imagine doing that. You're the guy. You know I'm obsessed with you."

"I'm not sure if the next rule is that you have to tell me every time," Pike said, "or that you have to never tell me. I'm still working on that."

"I'll await further instructions on rule four."

"The last one—if you do this, you have to look at addiction and compulsion, and really think about it."

"Come on, man. Don't go all shrink on me."

"I'm serious, Slater. You have to. Apparently there's an AA meeting in town for gay guys that's really regimented. Everyone has a task at each meeting. That might work for you."

"You researched this?" Slater demanded.

"A colleague at work mentioned it."

"So you're asking your coworkers how to deal with me."

"The discussion wasn't about you. He's a big twelve-stepper." Pike waved a hand. "If you don't want to do meetings, you have to read about it. I'll find a book or a website. You need to take stock of your behavior."

He'd heard that trope before, many times, from the shrinks, from Doris, from Andy. *Take stock* and *Take a good long look in the mirror* and *Check yourself before you wreck yourself.*

Slater gritted his teeth. "Fine."

"I want this to work," Pike said. "I want us to work. I feel like I'm compromising a lot."

"I know you are." He leaned toward him. "If it's any consolation, the fact that you give a shit about my well-being only makes you hotter."

Once they'd paid, and started walking back to his house on the quiet streets of his neighborhood, Pike briefly put his arm around his waist.

"So you can handle all that?"

"It'll be fine." Slater bumped his shoulder with his own.

"Should I write it all down? Maybe put it on a laminated wallet-size card for quick and easy reference?"

He laughed. "I'll remember. Besides, I don't think the written word is up to the task. Mere language can't really encompass what we have. If you tried to write about our narrative complex, you'd need six-dimensional paper."

"I get it. There's a lot going on." Pike swiveled his index finger around. "Even in directions you can't point."

"I love you with every fiber of my being," Slater said. "In all the dimensions."

Pike paused on the dark sidewalk and cradled Slater's face in his hands, and kissed him. "You're so intense," he said softly.

"Let me know if it's too much. I can probably track down some tranquilizers."

———·———

LATER, WHEN THEY WERE both undressed and got into bed, Slater caressed his chest.

"So I'm only allowed to fuck you."

"If you think you can pull it off."

Slater was already getting hard just from the feeling of his skin. Climbing up, he straddled him, and ground his woody into his thigh, then leaned in to kiss him.

"You're ready," Pike said, squeezing his cock.

Reaching for the bedside table, he grabbed a condom, and rolled it on. He locked his mouth on Pike's as he worked a finger inside him, then pulled back, and shoved his knees up, and penetrated him.

Pike's face contorted and he started panting as Slater built up to pounding him. Leaning over him, Slater squeezed his arms, then his pecs. When Pike met his gaze, Slater roared and climaxed. He sank on top of his body for a moment, mouthing his neck and breathing in the scent of his sweat.

Once he'd caught his breath, Slater shifted down and took him into his mouth. Pike quickly got hard, and Slater steadied him with a hand as he worked his cock. Groaning and straining into him, Pike came, his whole body shuddering.

Slater moved up the bed and stretched out beside him. He pulled Pike's arm under his neck, and leaned in to kiss him, then rolled onto his back.

"That was so fucking hot," Pike said. "Do you have any idea how hot that was?"

Slater hadn't had his taste yet, with the amber fifth still upstairs in the pantry, waiting patiently for him, but the mantle of sleep was already weighing on him.

"You're fucking hot," he mumbled.

NINE

WAKING IN BED, SLATER realized he was alone. When he got up his nose still hurt, throbbing anew to remind him how stupid he was, although it wasn't as painful as yesterday. He pulled on a pair of boxer shorts and went upstairs. Pike was in the kitchen, in his skivvies and a T-shirt, standing at the range with a spatula in hand.

"Flapjacks?" Pike said. "I found a vegan recipe."

"Right on." Stepping up behind him, he briefly wrapped his arms around Pike's torso, eliciting a laugh, and inhaled the heady scent of his sweat.

They carried their plates outside and ate at the patio table.

"I'm going in to the local office today," Pike said, setting his fork down.

"Is that in the Civic Center or in Westwood?"

"Christ, how many federal buildings are there?"

Slater waved a hand. "There's a few of them around."

97

"It's downtown."

"I can give you a ride."

"The bus goes right there," Pike said. "I checked."

"You'll need your earbuds."

"Why?"

"Trust me—you don't want to be on the bus without earbuds. I'm going to my office. I can drop you."

"Just let me take the bus. I want to see what it's like."

Once he'd had another coffee, Slater got dressed, and kissed Pike good-bye, and drove to the Fashion District. There were day laborers hanging out in the lobby of his building, and the elevator was crowded, the factories humming with the rhythm of sewing machines cycling on and off.

In his office the lights were on and the statue of Rey Pascual was facing the front desk. He knew Etta rotated him when she came and went, presumably so Rey could watch her work, and then watch the door when she wasn't in. That meant Etta was around.

When he stuck his head into Max's office, she and Max were parked on either side of his desk, both with stacks of paper in hand, and more paper piled on the desktop. It looked like printouts of spreadsheets.

"You're on a window-shade job?" Slater said.

"We're trying to find patterns in cell phone records," Max said. His eyes narrowed. "Did somebody pop you?"

Slater absently touched his nose. "Mary-Alice's ex. The guy who's not abusing his kid. At least he didn't break it."

"Are you done with that case?"

"I already wrote the report for her," Slater said.

"I'm kind of glad it was so straightforward—it gives me some free time. I have to buy a bed frame for the other bedroom."

Max laughed and sat back.

"What's so funny?" Slater demanded.

"When did you turn into a square? Shopping for furniture. No judgment, but it's a seismic shift in your priorities."

"He's right," Etta said. "You talk about furniture, and your mortgage, and love sweet love."

Slater frowned. "You make me sound so boring."

"It's just the opposite." She waved a hand. "Your narrative complex has energized you. Like hosing the garden to make the plants perk up."

"In school I did a whole unit on the Mojave Desert," he said. "The seeds of the native plants can lie dormant for ages when it's dry. Then when the winter rains come, or the summer monsoon, things spring to life. Not every seed, though. Nature is smart enough to reserve some to last through the next drought."

"There you go," Max said. "Pike is your monsoon."

"I suppose I am feeling energized these days."

Etta grinned. "As long as you haven't forgotten about work."

"I'm actually on a new job right now. Harold gave me a lead on this crypto guy that went missing. His business partner put a reward out for him. She was a child star from a kid show."

"Which one?" she said.

"I forget the name. Her name is Wilma, and so was the character's name."

"*Wilma's Walks?*"

"That's the one," Slater said. "Have you seen it?"

"I can't believe you haven't. Let me show you." She set her stack of paper on the edge of the desk and waved for Max to hand her the keyboard. Slater sat next to her in the other guest chair, and Max rotated the monitor so they could all watch.

Etta soon had a video clip playing. It started with chipper music and colorful titles.

"It's animated?" Slater said. "That means Wilma's not actually in it."

"Her voice is," Etta said.

An animated character, a little girl with dark hair, appeared on the screen.

"Let's go for a walk," she said, and beckoned the viewer to follow.

"It actually sounds like her," Slater said. "Even all these years later."

"It strikes me as odd that she went into the crypto business," Max said. "Why isn't she still an actor?"

"Harold said Lance did the coding to build the crypto product," Slater said. "I'm not sure how Wilma got involved. Maybe she was the one with the business savvy."

On the screen the animated Wilma spoke again. *"Vamos a caminar."*

"It's bilingual?" Max said.

Etta nodded. "It was one of the first. In education this was considered groundbreaking."

Wilma was pulling a red wagon now, and she looked at the viewers. "How many piggies are in the cart?" she said, and then repeated it in Spanish.

"Three," Slater snapped, and threw up his hands. "Fuck, Wilma, there's three fucking piggies. How can you be functional enough to speak two languages, and wander the countryside alone, but you can't count to fucking three?"

Frowning at him, Etta killed the video. "It's just a cartoon. It's for kids—it's supposed to be didactic."

Max laughed. "You should never have children."

"If this is the kind of trash they have to put up with, I never will." He waved at the screen. "Don't you think kids know they're being patronized?"

"They're children," Etta said. "You kind of have to patronize them."

A knock came at the front door.

"Are you expecting anyone?" Max said.

"Not me," Etta said.

Slater got up. "I'll check."

He pulled open the door a few inches, with his boot firmly planted against the inner side, in case someone tried to push their way in. It was Mary-Alice, and she scowled at the sight of him.

"What the hell, Slater?"

"What are you doing here?"

"You need to explain this." She waved a sheaf of letter-size paper.

"Is that my report? I thought it was self-explanatory. But we can talk about it, if that's what you need."

He pulled the door open and waved her into his office. Mary-Alice was wearing a dour gray suit again. She was probably on her lunch break from her oil company job.

Etta was standing in front of Max's office door, and it was closed now. That was smart—Mary-Alice was agitated, and she already knew Max. If she didn't know he was here, didn't get a glimpse of him, she wouldn't try to pull him into it.

"Can you bring me a coffee, honey?" Mary-Alice said to Etta. "Just black is fine."

"I'm not the help, sister," Etta snapped.

Slater had to suppress a smile. That happened to him all the time, as most of the manual labor and service work in this city was done by people who looked like him. But it was probably an unusual experience for Etta. He sat behind his desk, and waited for Mary-Alice to take the chair in front of it.

"Etta is one of our operatives," he said. "We don't have a coffee machine, but I could get you a glass of water from the sink in the latrine."

She wrinkled her nose. "No thanks." Flipping open her satchel, she pulled out the two flat cameras and tossed them on his desk. "Your microphones."

"I'm glad you found them both."

Mary-Alice waved the sheaf of paper again and slapped it on his desktop. "How could you say all this about Harold?"

"Whatever I wrote is what I saw. He changed the kid's diaper more than once, so I know she didn't come home loaded on Saturday."

"I told you I needed evidence of abuse."

"Harold talks to her and sings to her incessantly. That doesn't look like abuse to me. From what you told me I thought he was going to be a lowlife, but I really don't think he is."

"You were supposed to be the guy," Mary-Alice said. "I thought you could bend the truth a little."

Slater threw up his hands. "I wish you'd told me that when you hired me."

She scoffed. "I shouldn't have to spell it out."

"Well, I'm not psychic."

"Now that we're clear about what I need, can you rewrite this?" She tapped the paper on the desktop.

Slater sat back and watched her for a moment. "I lost my pop when I was thirteen. It kind of ruined me. Rose has this great father. What he's doing will make her smarter and happier. Why would you mess with that?"

"That's not the problem," she said intently.

"I'd think it would be valuable to have that kind of help. You get a day off once in a while. Harold is like free child care."

"You just don't get it." Mary-Alice rose, and stepped toward the door. "I'm disappointed in you."

"Join the club," he muttered, and sat up.

She turned back. "Pardon me?"

Slater raised his voice. "I said spare me the chin music, sister."

"You thought Harold was the lowlife, but it's you." She jabbed a finger at him. "You're the lowlife." And louder, "You."

She walked out, and Slater heard the front door close, then Etta stepped in.

"You heard all that?" Slater said.

"You left your door open." She shrugged. "I figured you wouldn't mind if I eavesdropped. Are you OK?"

"No skin off my nose. I'm not going to be her patsy. I just hope she doesn't make that kid any more miserable than necessary."

"She won't be able to fool the people at child and family services," Etta said. "They've seen it all before. And if the custody issue has already been through the courts, it won't be easy to get it back there."

"I hope so. In a way I guess Rose is lucky. There are two different people in this world who actually give a shit about her."

"I have to get to work," she said. "Call me if anything comes up."

"I assumed it wasn't a school day. What are you doing here?"

"It's a half day. I had the morning open."

Slater heard her talking to Max, and then the front door closed, and the deadbolt flipped as Etta twisted her key. Before he set to work, he eyed the statue of Pollux. Sweet Pike. He made the end of the day something to look forward to.

Grabbing his keyboard, he spent some time researching Wilma online. Max was right—it was an odd story. She was an ordinary kid from LA, a child actor with an ambitious stage mother. The acting work dried up, and a few years ago she'd started promoting NFTs for some artist friends, and that had led her to work for a crypto exchange. The exchange venture collapsed and took all the deposits with it. Wilma then teamed up with Lance Wiley, and they built their coin product in just a few months.

Max appeared in his office doorway.

"When Mary-Alice first came in here, she never said anything about cooking the report."

"You heard that?" Slater sat back. "I'm glad you think so. I thought maybe I'd missed something."

"The way I remember it, she was after the truth, not a hit piece. It usually works better for people if they explain what they actually want."

"Amen, brother."

"Anyway, I'm out."

Slater heard him bolt the door as he shifted his focus back to Lance and Wilma. Thinking it through, there wasn't really anyone else to interview about Lance. The front desk at Wilma's office, he remembered. Desiree. Maybe she'd been there long enough to remember Lance.

It would be easy enough to go back and talk to her at her office, but there'd been a membership card from that bougie gym on her desk. Pulling up a map, he looked for its locations. There was only one branch near that office. Some people worked out first thing in the morning, or after work, but maybe Desiree was the type who went at lunch.

Once he'd flicked off the lights and locked up, he went down to the street, and hustled across to his car, and drove to WeHo. Traffic was sluggish, and he had to troll for parking, but eventually he found a spot. Once he'd fed the meter, he walked back to the gym.

Beyond the front desk sprawled a big open room, brightly lit, with weight machines and bikes and treadmills. Even the gym equipment looked expensive. Almost right away he spotted Desiree. He had to grin—his hunch had been right. She was using an elliptical, wearing a stretchy blue top and black leggings, her hair tied back with a band. As the only not-white person in the room she was hard to miss. That wasn't just about the price point of the place— West Hollywood was extremely white.

The desk clerk was a buff guy in a tight red top that showed his nipples. He already had a wary eye on Slater. That was predictable—Slater wasn't dressed like their typical affluent clientele, and he was defi- nitely the wrong color for this place. If he tried to walk in and talk to Desiree, he'd instantly get waylaid, and interrogated, and frog-marched out to the street. Instead he waved at her, a wide motion with his whole arm. It worked—she noticed him, and her brow furrowed. But she didn't stop treading on the elliptical.

"Can I help you?" the desk clerk called to him.

Ignoring him, Slater pointed at Desiree and beckoned. Finally she stepped off the machine, and pulled a towel around her neck, and walked over.

"I remember you," she said. "You smacked a guy in the face even though he had a sidearm on his hip. What's your name again?"

"It's Slater. You certainly weren't afraid to get between us."

"I grew up in a house full of scrappy older brothers."

"That would explain it."

"Listen, Slater, I'm flattered. But I'm in a relationship right now."

He scowled. "I'm on dick, sister. I'm not looking for a date. This is business."

"What kind of business?"

He nodded to the desk clerk. The guy had his hands braced on the counter, not hiding the fact that he was tuned in to their conversation. "You really want to discuss that right here?"

"Fine. I'm done with my workout anyway. I'll grab a quick shower, and you can buy me a kombucha next door."

She walked away, and Slater looked the place over. It didn't seem that busy, but maybe that's what the steep membership fees bought, access to lots of open machines.

A guy clad head to toe in form-fitting athletic wear stepped up to the front counter and leaned on it, highlighting his impressive glutes. The desk clerk chatted with him, and laughed, and handed him something across the counter. Both were totally fuckable—it wasn't hard to imagine getting between them in the shower. He wondered what he'd have to say to talk them into it. Had he really given all that up? Maybe he did need a pocket-size quick-reference card for the new rules, like Pike had offered. Digging it out and reading it would pull his focus away from all that luscious man flesh.

TEN

WHEN DESIREE APPEARED, SHE'D changed into street clothes, a white blazer and tan trousers. Slater walked out with her, and into the kombucha bar next door. The interior was sleek and white, with lime-green shelves and a pink countertop. It didn't quite fit with trendy fermented tea—he'd expected hemp and sisal decor accented by splintery recycled two-by-fours.

"Get me a cinnamon piña colada," Desiree said. "I'll find a table."

She wouldn't have to look too hard, as there weren't many people in here. At the counter, the clerk tapped at the register as Slater recited her drink order, and perused the menu board for any of the other kombucha flavors that might be palatable.

"That's twenty-five even," the clerk said. "Anything else?"

"Dollars?" Slater said. "Are you fucking kidding me?"

The guy met his gaze, his brow furrowing. "It's a premium product."

"Give me a water too." He pulled out his wad, and peeled off a C-note, and met his gaze as he handed it over. "Tap water."

When he had the drinks in hand, he walked over to Desiree, parked at a table by the window. Setting them down, he sat across from her.

"Are you after the bounty?" Desiree said, and sipped at her straw.

"Private entities can't issue bounties. It's a reward. Lance was never charged with anything. There's no bounty."

Her brow furrowed. "OK, then, if you want to get technical about it."

"I'm interested in how and why Lance left the company."

"I was on a retreat upstate when he disappeared."

Slater nodded. "How long were you in for?"

"Just five days."

"At Chowchilla?"

"It was in Big Sur."

He frowned. "There's no prison there."

"What are you talking about?" she demanded.

"When you say you were 'on a retreat upstate' it means you were in prison. The women's prison is at Chowchilla. Nobody gets paroled after five days."

"I wasn't in prison." Desiree scoffed. "I was in the woods doing extreme yoga and getting my chakras power-washed."

"You were literally at a retreat."

She raised her eyebrows. "What did I just say?"

"Most of the people I deal with are lowlifes,"

he said, and gestured vaguely. "Going on a retreat is coded language. I never met anyone who went on an actual retreat."

"I am not a lowlife," she said intently.

"I get that. I can see that your chakras are really vibrant and lush right now. What exactly do you do for Wilma?"

"I deal with investors. Basically it's public relations."

"That's why they put you out front."

"Wilma calls me her fixer. Lots of times investors call when they're angry about their losses. My job is to smooth things out."

"What do you remember about Lance disappearing?"

"I'm not sure I should be gossiping about that."

"Don't get uptight," Slater said. "Just talk."

"I'm not uptight. It's internal company business." She waved a hand. "Blabbing about it probably violates my NDA."

"Wilma put up a reward. That means she wants people outside the company to know about all this."

She sipped at her drink. "I suppose I can't argue with that."

"Were they sleeping together, Lance and Wilma?"

"No way." She chuckled. "It was all business."

"What happened when he disappeared?"

"Lance was in the office one week, and then gone by the time I got back. Wilma was furious. She told everyone he took the company's money. But he was the company as much as she was. The thing nobody would say to her face, even though we all knew it, is that the company's assets were his as much as hers."

Slater nodded. "And you have no idea where he went?"

"I'm not sure that he went anywhere. Wilma can be pretty cold-blooded."

"You think she iced him?"

Desiree subtly glanced around the room and lowered her voice. "I think she buried his body in the Angeles National Forest, and snagged the money he took, and somehow moved it all to a tax shelter. Wyoming or South Dakota or the Cayman Islands. Or maybe she just lost it, like everyone else who invested in crypto." She met his gaze. "What I'm saying is, I don't think Lance is alive. That makes your bounty-hunting kind of pointless."

"Why would you work for a murderer?"

"I make good money." She shrugged. "Wilma needs me. She's not going to come for me."

"Is there anyone else I can talk to who was around back then? Former employees, maybe, or Lance's romantic partner?"

"I never heard of anyone like that."

"What about Wilma?" Slater said. "Does she have a husband or a wife?"

"Wilma doesn't do emotional stuff. I assume her sex life is battery powered. You might talk to the lawyer. Teresa. She was in the office all the time with both of them in those days."

"Does she still work with Wilma?"

"She moved on. I think she's at one of those white-shoe firms over on Fig."

"What's her surname?"

Desiree frowned in concentration for a moment, then snapped her fingers. "García."

Pulling out his phone, Slater thumb-typed the name into a note.

"Another person to talk to would be Miguel," she said. "He worked with both of them in the early days."

"Before the coin was created? How long was the company around before that?"

"It's been about three years total, leading up to and after the ICO. In crypto space that's a long time. Like thirty years in regular business."

"Where can I find Miguel?"

"He was Wilma's little brother on *Wilma's Walks*. He calls himself Brandon Fox these days."

"Is he still an actor?"

Desiree frowned. "He's *the* Brandon Fox."

"I've never heard of him."

"Well, other people have. It might be hard to get to him. He has a hit series right now. *Real Westside Reality Pros.*"

"That's reality TV?"

"It's a reality series about the people who make reality TV. Each of the characters works on a real reality series. But the show isn't real reality."

"So it's fake?" Slater demanded.

"It's reality, but it's scripted. That means there's a production schedule and studio time."

"What does Brandon's character do?"

"It's reality, so it's not a character. In the show he produces one of those reality chef shows," Desiree said. "It's called *America's Hottest Chefs.*"

"And that one is real reality."

"The show really exists. It's a crossover."

Slater took a breath to stifle an impatient retort.

"A crossover from what to what?"

"It's a competition show about spicy cooking, plus a dating show about the chefs' personal lives. It's clever, right? Hot food, hot romance. I think it's scripted too. Brandon doesn't actually work on the show, but in *Real Westside Reality Pros* he does."

"You're giving me a headache," Slater said. "But I think I get it. Brandon's series is called Real Westside what now?"

She repeated it slowly for him. "It's *Real Westside Reality Pros.*"

Once he'd thumb-typed a note of it, he met her gaze. "Is there anyone else who knew Lance?"

"There were some clerical staff, but they wouldn't know anything, and I wouldn't know their names." Desiree waved a hand. "It's a small office. A lot of the work was marketing, and lots of it was about people in other countries. Again, I have no idea who they were."

"All right." Slater stood up and tucked his phone away. "Enjoy your kombucha. It cost more than my shirt."

Out in the daylight, he walked back to the Thunderbird, and saw there was still some time on the parking meter. Once he was behind the wheel he looked up the lawyer that Desiree had named, Teresa García, on his phone. She really did work at a law firm on Fig, but she wasn't a partner. That was beneficial—it would be easier to get in to talk to her if she was lower down the ladder. Lawyers worked long hours, and it wasn't that late in the day. Teresa would still be in her office.

Next he did a search to find out where *Real*

Westside Reality Pros was filmed. It looked like it was in production now. In his contact list he found the number for a greenswoman he knew, Claudine, and dialed.

"It's been a minute," she said when she picked up.

"I know I'm no good at keeping up."

"Neither am I. Is this a social call?"

"It's work," Slater said. "There's a TV show that's filming this month at a studio in the Valley. I want to get on the green crew for a day or two, and I know you know that world."

"What's the show?"

"It's called *Real Westside Reality Pros*."

"I'm not even sure they have a green crew."

"I was told it's scripted."

"Let me ask around," Claudine said.

Slater ended the call, and started the engine, and nosed the Thunderbird into the traffic. When he got downtown, he pulled into the garage under the office tower on Figueroa where the lawyer worked. He could have phoned her, of course, but that would mean the rigamarole of explaining himself and making an appointment. That would take weeks. Walking in cold meant he could cut through a lot of the bullshit, and if she wasn't very important, it was less likely that he'd get blocked.

Up on the floor where her office was, he found the law firm's lobby. The walls were paneled in dark wood, like the furniture, with somber navy-blue upholstery. Whether the firm was historic and august or not, the decor was intended to give that impression. Farther inside he could see the more mundane reality, a few office doors on one side and bland beige cubicles filling the open space.

A tall *Dieffenbachia* stood next to the reception desk, staffed by a twenty-something guy wearing a dull red necktie. His sharp black hair was in tiny tight dreads, and his eyes flicked over Slater as he stepped in.

"Can I help you?" he said.

"You can help that plant." Slater gestured to it. "You need to repot it."

His brow furrowed. "Excuse me?"

"Your *Dieffenbachia* is root-bound."

"That's not really my department."

"You didn't kill anyone at the death camps," Slater said intently. "You just ran the points on the rail line. You just nailed up the barbed wire."

The guy sat back. "I'm not sure what you're talking about."

"Tell whoever takes care of the plants to deal with it. It's suffering, and that's on you. Also, I need to see Teresa García."

He took a breath. "Do you have an appointment?"

"I have information she'll want to hear. It's regarding a case she's working."

His eyes narrowed. "Teresa does contract law. She doesn't really work on 'cases.'" He waggled his fingers to put air quotes around the word.

"Man, just get her out here," Slater snapped.

Reaching for the phone, not taking his eyes off him, he tapped at the number pad, and spoke quietly into the receiver. Once he'd hung up he spoke.

"Would you like to have a seat?"

Slater put his hands on his hips. "No," he said flatly.

A woman walked out of the cube farm behind the reception desk. In her forties, maybe, she was curvy and wearing a tan outfit with a long sweater. Even though her name sounded Latin, she looked Asian, and wore her black hair pinned back, a chunky glass necklace at her collar. Her brow furrowed as she gave Slater a subtle once-over.

"Can I help you with something?"

Digging out a business card, he handed it to her.

"You're in insurance?" she said, studying it. "What is this about?"

"Two words," Slater said. "Lance Wiley."

"That was a long time ago."

"Can we talk in your office?"

Teresa glanced sidelong at the receptionist, who sat watching them closely. "I work in a cubicle."

"Is the conference room available? Lawyers always have one of those."

"There's a coffee place downstairs."

ELEVEN

ⅬⅬⅬⅬⅬⅬⅬⅬⅬ

SLATER FOLLOWED TERESA TO the elevators, and they boarded a crowded car to ride down. As he shuffled into a corner, his phone buzzed in his pocket, and he pulled it out to check. It was a text from Pike:

> Going for drinks with colleagues after work. Join us if you want.

A subsequent text had the name of a bar. He texted back a quick thumbs-up, then followed Teresa out to the street and into the open-air mall next door. The coffee joint was still open, even though twilight was looming, as it did so early in the winter. It was cool out but the place had little tables in the courtyard, far enough from the street that it was actually almost pleasant.

"Do you want a coffee?" Slater said.

"Get me a skinny latte."

Inside he ordered her an oat milk latte, and a

double espresso for himself, and carried them out to the courtyard.

"I can't really tell you anything about Lance," Teresa said, once he'd taken the chair across from her. She took a sip of her java. "I haven't seen him since he left. Why is an insurance investigator asking about him?"

"His name came up in a case," Slater said. "I can't get into the details. What did you do for his company?"

"The basic grunt work that lawyers do. I wasn't involved with the coin product directly. That was a dedicated team with crypto-specific knowledge. Half of them were in Slovenia or Slovakia or somewhere."

"Why did you leave that job?"

"After the third great crypto crash, the company downsized dramatically. There was no money for in-house counsel."

"My sense is that crypto is a grift," Slater said. "Would you say that's accurate?"

Teresa grinned and wrapped her hands around her cup. "That sounds like a philosophical question. It would take a smarter person than me to formulate a useful answer. Governments seem to think the traditional financial industry regulations will cover crypto, but that's like trying to read a web page with a telegraph machine. From what I've seen, personally, I wouldn't invest in it."

"You said Lance left. Other people have framed it that he disappeared."

"Lance is no sap. It's not like he'd get himself kidnapped or step off a cliff by mistake. He knew the outdoors. He'd go off camping by himself sometimes.

Up at Idyllwild and in the Anza wilderness."

"So you think he's still alive."

"I think he made himself disappear." She raised her eyebrows. "I think he's sitting pretty somewhere, drinking Coronas with his toes in the sand, looking up at the night sky. That was another of his extracurriculars—stargazing."

"What kind of guy was he?"

"You mean *is* he. He's not dead. I'd say Lance wasn't growth-driven the way a lot of entrepreneurs are. Wilma worked long hours and never complained, but Lance would leave the office at six with the lackeys."

"So he was lazy."

"Not that either." She frowned. "More like he was thoughtful. The guy came up with this product that absolutely blew up, and that was enough for him. Wilma believed it had to keep expanding indefinitely. That's the way corporate people run things. But Lance was content with the way things were."

"The product you're talking about is the coin they created."

"Right." Teresa sipped her coffee. "When you have a profitable business, you either have to keep growing it or sell it off. Lance didn't seem to want to do either. I'm sure the bankers and the brokers thought he was a fool."

"What about on a personal level?" Slater said. "Who was he dating? Who was he sleeping with?"

"No idea. I didn't know him all that well. Just around the office."

Slater nodded, thinking it through. "What do you mean when you call him thoughtful?"

"He thought about problems in alternative ways. I wondered if he was Buddhist or something, like my mother's people. I never asked him about that."

"Give me an example."

She shifted in her chair. "Well, a copyright issue came up. Some small-timer and a naming infringement. I was planning to send a cease-and-desist letter. It's standard practice. If they don't desist, you take the next step. Anyway, Lance says, 'Let it go, Teresa. They're never going to threaten what we've built.' That struck me as odd."

"Unprofessional?" Slater said.

"I'm sure the MBA crowd would say that. To me it felt like he was saying, 'Why put more misery out in the world?' That's why I wondered if it was a Buddhist thing."

"Someone told me they thought maybe Wilma iced him and buried his body in the forest."

Teresa smiled. "Wilma can be dogged, and ruthless, but I don't think she would have gone that far."

"That kid show thing, though. Doesn't that seem weird?" He mimicked the Wilma character: "'Let's go for a walk.' It kind of makes my skin crawl."

"Everyone comes from somewhere. That's where she's from."

"So why did Lance leave? Wilma says he ripped her off, and stole her money."

"That's confidential. Between attorney and client."

"This isn't a criminal case. It's office gossip." Slater gestured impatiently. "Sing, sister."

She frowned. "Did anyone ever tell you you're a little pushy?"

"I actually hear that a lot."

"I guess at this point it won't matter to either of them." She took a breath. "The partnership was deteriorating. Getting more acrimonious. They had divergent ideas about the future of the coin. I think Lance just got fed up. He didn't want to deal with the company or with the tax people."

"Did the company have tax problems?"

"Just Lance. I wasn't aware of it at the time, but after I left that job, these tax investigators came to interview me. They were looking for him." She raised her eyebrows. "Just like you are. Does he owe your company money or something?"

"That's confidential. Between investigator and employer."

Teresa chuckled, her eyes bright. "You're funny. Do you ever step out? Maybe we could grab dinner."

He slowly shook his head. "No way. I'm dick-exclusive."

"Well, that's something that I actually hear a lot. Are all the hot guys gay?"

"In a perfect world."

She rose and adjusted her sweater. "Nothing personal, but I hope you never find Lance. He's earned his peace."

Slater watched her leave, and drained his espresso, then walked back to the garage where the Thunderbird was parked.

He knew the place Pike had mentioned in his text. It was in the Civic Center, a pizza joint full of civil servants at lunchtime that morphed into a bar after office hours. Slater drove the few blocks east. It was late in the day, with the offices mostly cleared out, and he soon found a street space.

When he walked into the place, he spotted Pike sitting at the bar, twisted sideways on his stool, talking to a guy in a royal-blue dress shirt. He was leaning close to Pike. Slater paused to watch. He couldn't hear what they were saying, but as the guy spoke, he touched Pike's knee. Pike guffawed, tilting his head back. Slater could feel his heart pounding. Was this the guy who was handing out twelve-step recommendations? He gritted his teeth as he stalked over to them.

"Hey, Handsy," he said, looming over the guy. "Did you ever hear that thing about not pawing the merchandise?"

The guy eyed him and frowned. "The fuck are you?"

"I'm trouble," Slater said. "I'm the guy who's going to punch you in the face if you don't vacate pronto."

"Are you high?" he demanded, but slowly slid sideways off his stool and stood up.

Pike threw up a hand. "Slater, what the hell?"

"You know this guy?" Blue Shirt said.

"Hit the bricks, toots," Slater snapped, and jabbed a thumb toward the entrance.

The guy flashed his palms, and said, "Later, Pike," then strode out.

"What is wrong with you?" Pike demanded. "He's a work colleague."

"He was all over you."

"We were talking. I'm not going to sleep with him."

Slater put his hands on his hips. "Look me in the eye and tell me he wasn't trying to fuck you."

Pike scoffed. "You're a goddamn control freak,

you know that?" He stood up and strode toward the entrance.

"Where are you going?" Slater called after him.

He didn't answer, and disappeared onto the street. Was he following Blue Shirt?

There were a lot of eyes on him right now, Slater realized, glancing around the room. The bartender caught his eye and jutted his chin toward the door. Of course they didn't want a loud-mouthed hothead in here. He turned and walked out. On the sidewalk there was no sign of Pike or of Blue Shirt. Headed back to his car, he could feel the heat in his face. What had he just done?

He didn't notice at first that his phone was buzzing in his pants, but then he felt it, and pulled it out. It was Claudine, the greenswoman. He picked up and said, "Ibáñez."

"I called around," she said, "and I know who's doing that series. Can you meet the greensman tonight? He won't hire you without a face-to-face."

"I don't really need a job," Slater said. "I just need to go in on his crew."

"Still, he has to meet you first. You know the drill. I set up a meeting in half an hour. I know it's short notice, but that's when he's available."

"Who is this guy?"

"His name is *hy-mee*," she said, and spelled it, J-A-I-M-E, and gave him the name of a bar. "It's on Melrose, right by the freeway."

Climbing into the Thunderbird, he headed to East Hollywood. On the drive all he could think about was the fury in Pike's face, and the guy walking away from him, and the nauseating lump that had formed in his stomach. Should he call him now? It was probably too soon. He'd need time to simmer down. That's if he was ever going to talk to him again. If he hadn't picked up his stuff and left town for good.

Cruising past the place Claudine had sent him to, he saw a small sign for it over a narrow storefront. Once he'd parked, he walked back to it and stepped inside. It was a dive bar, with some worn black vinyl booths and padded barstools, permeated by the odor of cheap booze and the sweat of generations of alcoholics. The bartender was a woman with smoker's lines on her face and straw-dry peroxided hair tied up in a rough bundle. She called out a perfunctory greeting in a gravelly voice.

Claudine was here already, alone in a booth, absorbed in the hypnotic blue glow of her phone, and he walked over. There was more mileage on her since the last time he'd seen her, but she looked healthy. She must have been working today—clad in a red plaid shirt, her dark Latin hair was tied back in a utilitarian ball.

Claudine looked up and smiled as he approached the booth, and he slid in across from her.

"Thanks for arranging this," he said.

"It's the least I could do. You set me up with Svetlana, and she pays extremely well. It turned into an ongoing job. I'm doing the maintenance on her plantings."

"I'm glad that worked out. You know she's trouble, right?"

"I figured. I don't ask too many questions." Her brow furrowed. "You look a little shell-shocked."

Slater ran a hand through his hair. "I'm kind of

getting sticky with this guy. We just had a blow-up. I'm feeling sick to my stomach."

"What did you do?"

"Why do you assume it's something I did?" he demanded.

Claudine laughed. "I know you, remember?"

"Some sweaty desk jockey was macking on him in a bar. I eighty-sixed him, and Pike acts like I'm the asshole." Slater huffed. "Am I the asshole?"

"You know what they say—if you have to ask, it's probably you." She looked toward the entrance. "That's Jaime."

They both stood up as Jaime stepped over. In his fifties, he wasn't very tall, and had black hair and a thick mustache. His dark complexion implied that he worked outdoors a lot.

After Claudine had introduced them, Jaime said something to him in Spanish.

"Unfortunately I just have the one language," Slater said. "Is draft beer OK?"

He walked over to the bar, and ordered three smalls, and carried them back to the booth. The pair of them were talking in Spanish as he approached. He slid in next to Claudine, and they all tapped glasses.

Once he'd taken a sip, Jaime met his gaze. "So why do you want to be on my team for the filming?"

"I need to interview one of the actors."

"We call them participants."

"Of course," Slater said, raising his eyebrows. "It's reality TV. Nobody's acting."

Jaime laughed. "Which one is it? They're not all on set at the same time."

"Brandon Fox."

"I know he's on the shooting schedule tomorrow."

"Can we do it then?"

"Can you do any real work?"

"I've done some landscaping and gardening," Slater said.

Claudine waved a hand. "Don't let him under-sell it. We went to school together. Slater knows his stuff. I've seen him climb a fifty-foot *washingtonia* and trim it in a hot minute. Big old twenty-pound fronds raining down like flower petals."

"You can put me to work," Slater said, "but I'll have to stop when I get access to my target."

Jaime nodded. "So no *desmadre*."

"I don't know that word."

"You're not going to make a mess, and fuck things up."

"No way, brother."

"I'll see you in the morning," Jaime said, and tapped his glass to Slater's, then drained it. "Just don't embarrass me."

———◆———

PULLING UP TO HIS house, Slater saw the lights were on upstairs. Hopefully that meant Pike hadn't bugged out. Once he'd waited to make sure the garage door rolled all the way down, he hustled up the stairs, and found Pike on the sofa with his laptop. As he approached, Pike folded the computer closed, and set it aside. Slater knelt in front of him and gingerly put a hand on Pike's knee.

"I never wanted to hurt you."

"That's not what I'm pissed about," Pike said. "It's about being irrational."

"I warned you up front that I'm no damn good."

"Bullshit. You're not a bad person. You just act without thinking it through."

"The worst thing in the world is to have you angry at me. I'm broken, Pike. Damaged goods. Now you've seen my true colors." His voice broke, and he struggled to swallow the lump in his throat.

"Forget about that. It's just ..." He waved helplessly.

"I know," he said quietly.

"Can you see that being jealous of a work colleague is a little nuts?"

"Of course it's nuts. But he's hot, and the way he was looking at you, and touching you. He wanted you."

"That guy definitely doesn't want into my pants." Pike scoffed. "He's also far from hot. He's actually boring as dirt. He talks about his kids all the time. Even if he did want me, don't you think I could handle that on my own? I actually told him about you before you showed up. He texted me just now." Pike picked up his phone and read from it:

I hope you're making good choices.

"He sounds exactly like a dad," Slater said.

"It means he thinks you're a wastoid. What you did was how tweakers act when they're on a bender. You're lucky this guy is on the civilian side—he couldn't cap you. Lots of my colleagues are strapped."

"I hate that I upset you. That look on your face when you walked out of there. I can't stand it." Slater buried his head between Pike's knees, and Pike caressed his back, and they sat that way for a while.

Eventually Pike ruffled his hair. "That look on my face. What about the look on my face when I'm rock hard, and deep inside you, and making you scream. How do you feel about that one?"

Slater lifted his head. "I'd only be able to make a determination based on firsthand evidence. You'd have to demonstrate."

He chuckled, and they got up, and went down to the bedroom. Standing next to the bed, Slater wrapped his arms around him and pulled him close, relishing the vivid warmth of his body, the electric feeling of his hands on his back. He could feel Pike's cock swelling in his pants.

Pike pulled back, and his eyes narrowed, and he slapped him hard.

"Fuck," Slater roared, and moved to strike back.

Pike grabbed his wrist, and wrenched it down. Slater went with it, let himself be controlled.

"I'm going to have to teach you a lesson," Pike said.

Slater spoke through his teeth. "Bring it on."

He shoved Slater onto the bed, and straddled him, then unbuckled his belt and yanked down his jeans. Slater watched as Pike ditched his trousers and pulled off his shirt. As advertised, he was rock hard. When they were both naked, Pike took a minute to roll on a condom, then climbed up, and straddled his pelvis, and slapped him hard enough to turn his head.

"Spread out," Slater snapped, and glared at him, but didn't strike back.

Pulling back, Pike reached between his legs and probed him, then leaned into his mouth, exploring with his tongue, warm and intent. Shifting closer,

Pike pushed up his knees and penetrated him. He started slow, and built up speed, looming over Slater. He slapped him again, and Slater slapped back.

"Fuck you," Pike growled, pounding him now. "You fucking psycho."

Slater slapped him again, and Pike yelped, and climaxed, and sank on top of him. When he rolled off, he mouthed Slater's neck, and his jaw, and stroked him for the brief moment it took until he came.

A while later Pike rose, and he heard the shower go on. When he came back he handed Slater a towel. He'd get up in a minute for a snort of his quotidian applejack, but for right now the proximity to Pike felt magnetic, and it was all he wanted. Pike lay down, and Slater prodded him to shift onto his side, then wrapped an arm around his warm damp chest, and notched his knees into his. There was no better feeling in the world than this.

TWELVE

WAKING BEFORE HIS ALARM, when it was still dark out, Slater sat up so that he wouldn't drift off again. Pike didn't stir, and for a minute he watched him sleeping, all slack-jawed and innocent. A flash of guilt struck him then, remembering Pike's angry face when he walked out of that bar.

"You're so fucking beautiful," he whispered.

He got dressed as quietly as he could, and didn't bother going upstairs for coffee, instead heading down to the garage, and drove to the address Jaime had given him in East Hollywood.

It was near where they'd met last night, in the rolling hilly neighborhood south of the freeway, and Slater found a place to park on the crowded street. At Jaime's house there was a box truck in the drive-way. The top was open, he saw, and covered with half-shade mesh cloth. Inside sat an array of boxed and potted plants.

When he walked up, Jaime greeted him with a big smile.

"I take it you're a morning person," Slater said.

"Jump in," Jaime said. "I'm ready to roll."

"Where's your crew?"

"There's not a lot of green work today. It's just you and me."

Slater climbed in the passenger side, and Jaime backed into the street and navigated the truck onto the 101, taking the turns slow.

"So you spy on people for a living?"

"Mostly I work insurance fraud cases," Slater said. "Sometimes it's hard to interview people. When they're celebrities, like this guy, they have layers insulating them from the world. Agents and representatives and assistants."

"Brandon is a pretty big name. In this series he's one of the top participants."

Traffic was light so early in the day, and they rolled into the Valley, and pulled up at the studio gate. The guard waved them through, and Jaime drove slowly in the wide aisles between the buildings. It looked like a substantial facility. Lots of film production had moved out here, and then moved even farther out when they needed more room. But the industry had never really vacated any of the old neighborhoods, and there were still studios and production facilities large and small all over the metropolis.

"We're doing two scenes in the morning and two in the afternoon," Jaime said. "In the morning both scenes are outdoors. After lunch it's on the set that's supposed to be their office, where the participants all make the reality TV shows."

"But it's just a sound stage."

"The first one is filming a sidewalk scene. The participants are talking on the street outside a restaurant. I'm thinking we'll use the camellia. It's blooming right now."

He stopped the truck near a set that was built to look like the brick wall of a building, but it was just a few feet thick, and braced on the back with scaffolding. As they climbed out Slater looked it over. There was a stretch of sidewalk in front of the wall, and a curb, and parking meters.

It looked like an ordinary street in the city, but it must have been cheaper to rebuild it here. Or maybe it was cheaper because they didn't need a permit, like they would on location, or a security team to chase off the homeless, or someone to hose away the urine stains on the sidewalk, or scrub off the graffiti, or sweep up the garbage. On second thought, it was obvious why they'd rebuilt it here—they were feeding the fantasy. This is what a street would look like in a functional society.

Jaime stepped next to him and nodded to a small group of people nearby. A woman in a plaid shirt and jeans held a portable camera on her shoulder, and a skinny guy with his hair in a rattail had a pole with a big fuzzy mike at the end.

"The gray-haired guy is Marty," Jaime said quietly. "He's the director. That's Brandon and Shawna. Both of them are participants."

It was easy to see which ones he meant—Marty's gray mane was tucked under a ball cap embroidered with BOSS, and Brandon and Shawna were the only ones wearing stage makeup.

"In this series Brandon works on a reality chef show," Jaime went on, "and Shawna works on a makeover show."

"But they don't really work on those shows."

"Not Brandon, but Shawna really does work on the makeover show. They do cosmetic surgery on ugly people so that they can get married and be happy. It's called *Fuggly to Fabu.*"

"What an uplifting gift to the world," Slater said. "How many participants are there on this series?"

"Maybe eight or ten? I get the scripts a few days ahead. Today it's just these two. We're filming a couple of romantic scenes on small sets. That's why I don't need a lot of help."

Jaime walked back toward the truck, and Slater watched the crew. Despite his whitewashed name, Brandon still looked Latin. He wasn't very tall, and he looked buff, with carefully coiffed black hair. His outfit must be intended to look office-casual—chinos and a plain collared shirt.

Shawna was rail-thin and had an expensively coiffed blond mane. She was a little young for surgery, and if she'd had any herself, it was subtle. She'd flicked her hair away from her face several times since he'd been observing them. Was it a nervous tic, or part of the character? The elaborate coiffure didn't quite mesh with her bland clothes—capri pants and pumps, and a sweater draped over a dress shirt that emphasized her abundant breasts. No way were those real, so out of proportion with her frame.

Jaime called to him from the truck, and Slater walked over. He was standing in the bed and had the lift gate folded out.

"Let's move the camellia," he said.

Slater climbed up and helped him drag the heavy boxed plant onto the lift. It was in great shape, he saw, straightening up. Maybe seven feet tall, it had been well-tended, and there were lots of blooms. But it hadn't been turned into a topiary mess. Jaime clearly knew what he was doing.

"Grab the handcart." Jaime gestured farther inside.

Once Slater had rolled it onto the gate, Jaime pressed the handle to lower them all to the ground.

"There's a green marker where they want it," he said, pointing toward the brick wall.

Slater tucked the handcart under the camellia's box and tentatively lifted it. It didn't overbalance, and it wasn't actually that heavy with wheels under it. Moving slow so as not to shock the plant, he wheeled it over to the wall. Sure enough there was a green X spray-painted on the fake sidewalk. He positioned the box over the mark and set it down.

The director, Marty, stepped over and stood a few feet away, soon joined by his participants—Brandon and hair-flicking Shawna. They weren't paying attention to him, looking at the set and talking about the scene. Slater squatted to adjust the plant box so that it was parallel to the wall, and Marty gestured to it.

"Maybe Shawna could pick a rose and offer it to Brandon."

Slater eyed him as he stood erect. "These aren't roses."

Marty frowned. "Excuse me?"

"I said these aren't roses."

"I heard you. I think I know what a rose looks like."

"They're camellias. They don't have stems. If you pick one, you'll have to hold it cupped in your hand." He mimed the action with an upturned palm.

"They look like peonies to me," Shawn said. "Miniature ones."

"Peonies don't grow in this climate, and they don't grow on shrubs." Slater frowned. "What planet are you from?"

Jaime stepped up and put a hand on Slater's shoulder. "Pick the camellias if you need them," he said to Marty.

Marty's brow furrowed. "You're sure they're not roses?"

Jaime pulled Slater away, toward the truck, and spoke under his breath. "Chill, *vato*. They don't want to hear anything from us."

"Got it," Slater said. "No *desmadre*."

"I'm going to stay here. Can you move the truck?" Jaime pointed to a hulking studio building. "Go that way. Out into the lane, turn right, then back it in on the set that looks like the front door of an apartment building. There's a yellow line where the end of the box needs to be. You have to drive slow."

"Keys?" Slater said, and once Jaime had handed them over, he took a minute to stow the lift gate in its vertical position, then climbed in the cab and started the engine. He pulled away gently, knowing what was in the back, and shifted into second gear, but drove slowly, the way Jaime had on the way in.

The set was where Jaime said it would be, a double glass door and a section of stuccoed wall with house numbers attached. Like the other set, it was just a few feet thick, and he could see right through the doors to the asphalt lot behind. The camera must film it at an angle to avoid revealing that view. That was the magic of this business, he realized. Not-quite-real reality. They could take all this fake temporary stuff and turn it into something that looked believable.

No one was around this set yet, and as he drove closer he spotted the yellow line, and backed the truck up to it, and killed the engine.

There was no point in watching them desecrate that camellia back at the other set, he knew, as he wouldn't get a chance to corner Brandon while he was being filmed. Instead he sat in the truck and looked at his phone.

He'd been dozing, he realized, when his phone buzzed in his hand and he started awake. It was a text from Pike:

> In case you're looking for me later, I'm going to Bakersfield for the day. Pawn shops! I'll see you this eve.

Lots of firearms got sold through hock shops, he knew. That must be what Pike was up to, tracking down a weapons sale or knocking pawn brokers' heads together. He sent a terse reply:

> I'll fuck you this eve.

A moment later Pike's response made him smile: a GIF of a dachshund nodding its head, superimposed with the word SOON.

Climbing out of the cab, he tucked his phone away and walked back to where the boxed camellia was. It had been a while—they weren't filming anything now, and none of the crew were in sight. There was no sign of Jaime either, but the handcart was here. He was considering whether he should reclaim the camellia and walk it over to the truck when the blond stepped up.

"Hey, greensman," she said. "I'm Shawna."

"I know. *Flabby to Fabu*."

"It's *Fuggly to Fabu*." Her brow furrowed. "I know you know that. Can I give you a piece of advice?"

"When has that question ever worked out well for you?" Slater demanded.

"If you're going to make it in this business, you need to respect the luminaries."

He put his hands on his hips. "That would be you, and the other actors?"

"We're called participants. I'm talking about the director."

"You mean the thing about the camellia bush? I should have said, 'Yes, sir, this is definitely a rose?'"

"Marty's important to this TV station. He deserves respect."

"I thought this was a film studio."

"It's a TV studio. Channel 6. Marty has been here for almost a decade. He built this station into what it is today. From the ground up. With his bare hands."

"I get it," Slater said. "He did the framing, and put up the drywall, and climbed Mount Wilson with the transmitter on his back."

Shawna raised her eyebrows and flicked her hair back with her nails. "Practically, yes."

He knew he had to put up with this, knew he couldn't clap back and embarrass Jaime. He dug deep, for material from the shrinks of his youth, the phrases they'd trained him to say to mollify people.

"Thank you for your insight, Shawna," he said. "You've given me a lot to think about."

She nodded. From the look on her face, that had been the right thing to say.

"You'll get there," she said. "Just keep striving."

Biting his tongue, Slater walked over to the other set, where the truck was parked. Jaime was here now, standing in the back, with the gate folded horizontal.

"Should I move the camellia over here?" he called up to him.

"They're not done with it," Jaime said. "We can do that at the end of the day."

"No one is going to jack it?"

"Not here. If they do, it goes on my invoice to the production company. Right now we need to move two podocarps out of the truck. Can you get the handcart?"

Slater hustled back to the other set, and returned rolling the cart in front of him. Jaime already had the podocarps on the lift gate. They were tall but the boxes were smaller than the camellia's. As Slater trotted up, Jaime lowered the gate.

"We need to set them on either side of the set's doorway," Jaime said. "Spaced so that it looks natural."

Sliding the handcart under one of the boxes, Slater gently tilted it up and pulled it over to the faux building facade. Once he'd set it down, Jaime took the cart and went to the truck for the other one. They positioned them on either side of the doorway, and Jaime looked them over.

"Can you make sure they're even with the door?" Jaime said, and rolled the handcart back toward the truck.

Slater crouched to shift one of the boxes a few inches so they'd both be the same distance from the wall, then rose and took a step back to make sure.

Marty, the director, was here now, and called to him.

"Greensman, is that the best face toward me? We need the best face toward the camera. Do both of them."

"Let me check," Slater said.

He knew damn well Jaime took good care of these, and rotated them regularly to get even sun exposure and uniform growth. Every side had the same luxuriant lush foliage. Even so, he spent a minute studying them, stepping around the plants and furrowing his brow in concentration. Eventually he stooped and twisted each of the boxes ninety degrees. Marty had walked away. Obviously what mattered wasn't how the plants looked, but that he was following orders.

Jaime was standing nearby, arms folded, a trace of a grin on his face, and Slater stepped over.

"I think I found the best face," he said, "but you might want to check my work."

Jaime laughed. "You have to play along. It's like in the military. He's the boss. It doesn't matter how pointless it sounds—you just do what you're told."

"Those podocarps are beautiful from any side. I know you know what you're doing."

"Only the best for the small screen."

Marty returned, and more people gathered around him, the woman with the camera and the mike-boom guy and a couple of people staring at tablet screens. Shawna and Brandon were in completely different outfits now, although both still looked bland and business-casual. Slater walked back toward the truck, following Jaime.

"It's not going to fucking work," someone shouted, and Slater stopped to look. It was Brandon, standing with the director. He lowered his voice, and Slater couldn't hear the rest of the conversation, but he watched the two of them interact. There was a lot of arm-waving.

Jaime stepped up beside him and spoke quietly. "Is he on meth?"

"I was thinking that too. Tweakers definitely act like that."

"They think no one can tell."

"You know, actors can be intense like that even without meth," Slater said. "Maybe he's sober."

Eventually Brandon walked away and went around behind the fake stucco facade. The camera operator lifted the device to her shoulder, and the guy with the mike took a position near the podocarps.

Marty called "Action," and a moment later Brandon strutted out through the fake front door. Shawna stepped in from the side and stood in front of him.

"Have you got a problem with me?" she demanded.

"Cut," Marty shouted. "Shawna, that was absolutely perfect. Your training shines through like a golden beam in the darkness. But we need more body language—can you use your hands? Remember that you're upset."

Shawna nodded and stepped back to where she'd started from. Brandon went back through the doors, and strutted out through them exactly the way he had the first time. As she stepped up, Shawna lunged at him in a feint, throwing her hands in the air.

"Have you got a problem with me?" she shouted, much louder than before.

"I don't have a problem," Brandon shouted, and jabbed a finger at her. "It's you. You've got a problem."

"I hate you," Shawna shrieked, in a tone that made Slater's ears ring, and ran off camera.

"Let's try it once more," Marty called out.

Shawna resumed her ready position, flicking her hair out of her eyes. She did that so often. Had no one ever told her about hairspray? Maybe he should return the favor and give her a piece of advice.

They ran through the scene again. Brandon instantly ramped up from calm to shouting, just the same as before, like he'd flipped a switch. Maybe he wasn't on meth, Slater decided. His range of emotion was too fluid. The guy was actually a pretty competent actor.

Finally Marty called, "Scene," and everyone clapped.

"They got it in two takes?" Slater said to Jaime.

"It was three."

"That doesn't leave a lot of room for error."

"On movies they do a dozen or more," Jaime said, "but this is reality."

"Of course," Slater said. "You want to keep it real."

"I'll ask if they're done with the outdoor scenes. We can put the podocarps back on the truck."

Watching the crew, he saw Brandon walk over to one of the trailers parked at the side of the space, and step inside.

"I'm afraid you're on your own," Slater said. "I see an opportunity to talk to my target."

THIRTEEN

S TRIDING OVER TO THE trailer, Slater saw that it had a star emblazoned on the door with BRANDON FOX written across it. He knocked, and pulled it open, and stepped in. Brandon was on the sofa.

"This is a private dressing room," he said, and frowned.

"I just need a minute of your time."

"Aren't you the 'camellias aren't roses' guy?"

"They're not," Slater said, "despite what you want to believe. They're not even in the same order. Unlike reality television, in actual reality the truth is immutable."

"It was a good call. We tried it, and then did the scene without it. It looks stupid to hand someone a flower with no stem."

"The poets speak in beautiful verses, but they don't have wisdom."

"What does that mean?" Brandon said.

"Just that I told your nebbishy dipshit director that it wouldn't work, and he didn't believe me."

"His name is Marty. Who's the poet?"

"Marty. You. Kinematic people." He gestured helplessly. "I've been reading the classics."

"Marty says *Skanky Housewives* season one is the classic in our genre. It really burned bright. It must have won a dozen Emmys. Where did you find the script?"

"Listen, Brandon, I'm trying to track down Lance Wiley. You worked with him."

"That's a long time ago." His eyes narrowed. "What's that got to do with gardening?"

"You know he went missing, right? Have you got any idea where he might be?"

"None."

"Do you think Wilma iced him?"

Brandon scoffed. "If she had, she wouldn't have been looking for him so hard."

"She's been doing that recently?"

"In the fall I know she hired a couple of down-low Russian PIs to hunt for him in Europe."

"She said she did that, or she actually did that?"

"One of the old crowd told me about the Russkies, and I asked Wilma about it when I talked to her. She told me to keep it quiet."

"Who was the person you talked to?" Slater said.

"Her fixer. Desiree. I think she's on the front desk now."

"Is Wilma the type who'd murder somebody?"

"I've known her since we were both in grade school," Brandon said. "We worked on our first series together."

"That's not an answer."

"Wilma wants to get her hands on the assets Lance took with him. It was over a billion dollars at the time."

"I was told Lance didn't actually take money. He took the coin product."

"'Coin' means money—the coin is the money. Although the exchange rate is probably a fraction of what it was since the last crypto meltdown."

"Crypto isn't money," Slater said. "It's an intangible financial asset with nothing backing it up."

"You sound like a skeptic." He waved a hand. "Whatever you call it, he took the coin. In Wilma's mind it was the same as money."

"It was worth a billion dollars, you said. Was that the value of the entire coin? How is Wilma still in business?"

"He took half of what they created, so it must have been worth two billion total."

"If it was half his creation," Slater said, "half his company, didn't he have a right to it?"

"That's not how Wilma sees it." Brandon gestured helplessly. "I don't think she'll ever find him."

"Why is that?"

"He's probably working with the Russian hackers. I think that's why she hired Russians to find him. It's the only scenario that fits. Lance is in a bunker in St. Petersburg. He disappeared so he could go help them plunder more coin."

"Did he have connections in St. Petersburg?"

"Not that I know of. He was good at coding. Fast and accurate, I was told. That's what all those coins are based on. It's just software."

His belt was at Brandon's eye level, and the guy was looking at his crotch, he realized. His gaze lingered just a moment too long.

"You see something you like down there?" Slater said, and put his hands on his hips.

"I like those jeans," he said, and shifted uncomfortably.

"I can show you what's in them, if you want." Technically Pike was out of town, so it fit with the new sex rules.

Brandon shook his head. "I don't have any money."

"I'm not turning tricks, you punk," Slater said sharply.

"Don't get steamed. A lot of people on set are selling something. Mostly drugs or sex."

"You're hot, Brandon. It's undeniable. It's why they put you on television. I'll fuck you, if that's what you want."

"What is it about blue-collar guys?" He rose and stepped close to Slater, and grabbed his waist, and pulled him close.

"You've got wood," Slater said.

"Do you want a bump before we get into it?"

"No," he said flatly, "and if you're already high, I'm leaving."

"Such a hard-ass. I think maybe you need to show me who's boss." Still grasping his belt, Brandon winced and turned his head. "But not the face."

"You don't want me to mess up your stage make-up?"

"I can't kiss you."

He didn't need to kiss him. Slater nuzzled his neck, and unbuttoned his shirt, and mouthed his chest. Shoving him onto the sofa, Slater pushed his feet apart with his boots. His eyes bright, Brandon gasped and moved to unbuckle his belt. Slater knelt between his knees and swatted his hand away, then quickly undid his pants, and yanked them partway down, and took him into his mouth.

Brandon was fully hard, and moaned as Slater got into it, and guided him with a hand on his head. Slater smoked him until he came.

He pulled back, and once Brandon's breathing had slowed, he sat up.

"On your feet. Let me do you."

"Can I sit down?" Slater said.

"It's hotter if you're standing." He knelt in front of Slater and unbuckled his belt, then yanked open his jeans and pulled out his cock.

As Brandon went down on him, grasping his thighs, Slater groaned with the intense sensation. If the guy was filming more scenes today, he didn't want to muss his hair, and instead braced his hand on the wall. Leaning into him, Slater soon climaxed.

Grinning and red-faced, Brandon sat back on the sofa. "That was fun. A blow job at lunch break."

"Maybe you'll have clearer focus this afternoon," he said, as he buttoned his fly.

"You can hang out if you want. I'm not due on set again for a little while. That rock is still on offer if you want a hit."

"You're actually a fairly skilled actor," Slater said. "You should try working sober."

He stepped out onto the lot, wincing at the bright daylight, and closed the door. As he walked toward Jaime's truck, Shawna stepped out of an identical trailer, parked in front of Brandon's, and walked toward him.

Meeting his eye, she laughed. "Oh, this is good."

Slater paused and frowned. "What are you talking about?"

"You've got body makeup all over your face."

Dabbing at his cheek, he examined his finger. "It must be pollen from the camellia."

"That's a lie. There's only one person who wears makeup that pale. I get it—you're kind of his type."

"Listen, toots, I don't know what you're talking about. All I'm hearing right now are baseless rumors and innuendo."

He walked away, and at the truck found Jaime, with the lift gate set at chair height, sitting on it and eating a tamale. He frowned as Slater approached.

"What's on your face?"

"I'm not sure."

"Well, that's strange. Did you bring lunch?"

"I got what I came for, so I'm leaving," Slater said. "Unless you need me."

Jaime raised his eyebrows. "It's just a few plants. I think I can manage."

"I appreciate you helping me get on the set."

"I enjoyed watching you school Marty on the greenery. I could never get away with that myself."

"Will it blow back on you?" Slater said. "I wasn't really trying to argue with him."

"There are some very fragile egos in this business. If it comes up I'll tell them I fired you for your unruly attitude."

He scoffed. "I can't believe you have to put up with stuff like that. I hope they pay you well."

"I'm on Hollywood lira like everybody else."

"They don't pay you in greenbacks?"

"Lira just means well paid. Hollywood budgets have an extra zero or two compared to real-world budgets."

"You're saying that you're making bank."

Jaime waved a hand. "How much would you charge for that boxed camellia?"

"It's in great shape," Slater said. "Maybe three hundred."

"That's what I'd charge for it out in the real world. If they don't return it to me, I'll invoice for it with an extra zero. Three grand. On paper it looks more like lira than dollars."

"Maybe I need to get into your business."

"You'd have to lose the attitude first."

Slater nodded. "I've heard that all my life."

——·——

THERE WAS A METRO line near here, Slater knew, and as he walked toward the studio gate he checked the map on his phone for the nearest stop. Rather than a train it was a half-ass dedicated bus line built on a railroad right-of-way. In their wisdom Valley politicians had made it illegal to build rail transit out here. They must have really enjoyed sitting in traffic. More likely it was a way to prevent brown folks from getting easy access to the neighborhood. If so it had been a futile maneuver—they'd moved out here anyway.

He boarded the bus and found a seat next to the window, and settled in, watching the urban landscape roll by. Brandon's version of Lance's departure didn't line up with Wilma's, or with all the gossip online. If he was telling the truth about Wilma hiring PIs on the down-low to look for Lance, that implied it wasn't just for show, that she hadn't actually iced the guy. But Brandon could be colluding with Wilma, spinning her disinformation. The best evidence that Wilma really was still looking for Lance was that she was harassing somebody outside her orbit about it—Harold.

Once he'd transferred to the train, it was just a few minutes' ride back to Hollywood, and he walked from the station on Vermont to his car. Heading downtown, he parked in the surface lot behind Andy's place. Andy had told him to call first, but he wasn't just going to roll over and acquiesce to that new rule. It felt pushy. No way was he about to let Andy freeze him out.

The building was an old textile warehouse that had been renovated as lofts, with the original wooden floors and multipane windows. When he went up to his floor and knocked on the door, Andy pulled it open. Even in winter he ran hot because of his CP, and today he was wearing his usual tank top and boxer shorts. Lithe and with taut muscle tone, his hair was a perfect tousled mess.

"What are you doing here?"

"Last time you told me I couldn't see you," Slater said. "What's up with that?"

"What's on your face?"

"Camellia dust. I was moving some plants around."

"Were you motorboating them?"

He waved an arm. "Can I come in?"

"Is this work-related?"

"Does it matter?" Slater demanded.

Andy sighed and stepped inside, walking with his characteristic uneven gait, and dropped into his desk chair. The loft was mostly one room, with a bed and a computer desk and a compact kitchen table under the oversize windows.

"What's the job?" Andy said.

"How do you feel about missing persons?"

"Are the police … looking for them? I'm not going to mess with an … official investigation."

"Law enforcement isn't involved. He disappeared by choice."

"Sit down," Andy said, and waved to the table.

Slater pulled out a chair and sat facing him.

"That work is called … skip tracing. Looking for people who … don't want to be found."

"I've heard that term before. It's how they look for deadbeats."

"It's a specialized skill, and I don't … really do it. But I can take a poke at it. Most people leave … more tracks than they think they do."

Slater told him about Lance, and the company he'd built with Wilma, and how he'd disappeared with the crypto. He pulled out his phone and sent him links to a couple of articles about Lance.

"I'm not sure I'll be able to find … anything, whether he's alive or not," Andy said. "Rich people can disappear more effectively than … the rest of us. Buy a new passport and … poof, you're gone."

"I get it. Just let me know what you find." He raised his eyebrows. "Do you have time to mess around?"

"No monkey business. I've got … stuff to do." He waved his arm. "Get out of here."

"Can I kiss you," Slater demanded, "or is that too simian?"

"Fine," he said flatly.

Dropping to one knee in front of him, Slater leaned in, and met his warm lips, and lingered in it. When he pulled back, he studied Andy's face. Something was different these days. Like a wall was going up.

"Bye, beautiful," he said, and got up, and walked out.

That look in Andy's eyes. Thinking about it made him feel a little queasy. Resignation, it had looked like, and maybe sadness too. Andy had been pissed at him for getting with Pike. He never meant to hurt the guy, but it was inevitable—it was the ancillary carnage of Slater's crazy life.

———•———

ONCE SLATER GOT BACK to his house, he went upstairs and took a shower to wash off the body makeup, then changed into sweatpants and a T-shirt. When Pike arrived he embraced him and kissed his neck.

"How was B-field?"

"Flat," Pike said. "The agents who work there call it Bake-oh. I won't say it's the Paris of North America."

"There's more oil wells than Paris, though."

Slater squeezed him tighter for a moment, and Pike swatted his butt.

"The sweatpants suggest we're in for the night."

"I can order Thai."

Once Pike had changed out of his work drag, and the food came, they ate at the dining table. Pike told him more about B-field, and the hock shops, and Slater talked about his case. Eventually sated, he pushed his plate away.

"Wilma really wants to find this guy, and that makes me really want to find this guy, so I can claim all that lettuce."

"You're sure what's between her and Lance is just about money?" Pike said. "Not a personal beef?"

"It's corporate-level money. Someone told me north of a billion dollars."

"That would definitely incite her to play hardball. And it explains the absurdly high reward."

"Can you check into Lance for me in your government databases?"

Pike frowned. "I can't dig into case files for you."

"I don't need anything confidential. Just tell me what's public record about him. He's been missing for a while. Does he have any warrants, is he on any watch lists? I figured you could save me some time and not break any of your laws."

"The law actually applies to you too." He furrowed his brow. "It's not a great precedent. But text me the name."

That was all Slater needed to hear. He pulled out his phone and tapped at it.

After he'd stowed the leftovers in the icebox, they got comfortable together on the couch, with Pike leaning back on him, and Slater resting a hand on his chest. He read from the book they'd been sharing, following Aeneas as he traveled deeper into the underworld.

Eventually Slater set the book down. "I like the idea of the Lethe. Can you imagine a river that made you forget everything? If you could bottle it, you'd make a mint. Instant PTSD remover."

Pike didn't respond, and Slater cocked his head to look at him. The guy was awake, staring absently out the French doors at the dark city.

Slater snapped his fingers. "Planet Earth calling Pike."

Pike chuckled, and sat up, turning to face him.

"What's going on?"

"You're a million miles away," Slater said. "What's up?"

"I guess we have to talk about it eventually."

He tossed the book onto the coffee table. "Spill it," he demanded.

"They move us around a lot," Pike said. "I've been seconded a couple times. It's part of the deal. I kind of clicked with the people on that Bake-oh run. I could easily get onto a team in LA."

"Would that be a good career move for you?"

He raised his eyebrows. "It would."

"You can live here," Slater said. "You already have a key. Use the spare bedroom as your office. That way Doris can't warehouse her out-of-town visitors here. Win-win for me. I don't want your animal products hogging up the Frigidaire, though. You can have one shelf."

Pike laughed. "It's more than that. It's intense to live together. A huge step."

"I never get tired of you. If you were always in town I wouldn't have to fuck anyone else. You'd be my live-in squeeze."

"That's so eloquent, petal. So sentimental and romantic."

"I know it sounds a little louche, but you know what I mean. You just read me the riot act this week."

"The big thing is my family," Pike said. "I'm not sure I want to be so far from them. I need to think it through."

"You can go back there as often as you come here now. I'd still contribute to your air travel costs."

"So you're totally down with the possibility."

"No question, no hesitation," Slater said. "Also no demands. I want you here, as much as you want to be. If it doesn't happen, I want you anyway—as much of you as I can get."

Pike leaned in and kissed his neck, then shifted to get comfortable in his arms. They lay that way for a while, and he clung to the warmth of Pike's body. He couldn't get enough of that, and the feeling of his skin. It felt like it was recharging him.

"Maybe I'll join you in your nightly snort," Pike said, and got up.

Slater followed him to the kitchen, where he pulled open the pantry cupboard.

"If you're drinking too, we should have the good stuff," he said.

The guy bought decent scotch, and left a bottle here, but it was too pricey to be everyday booze. Pike took out the fifth of Slater's cheap bourbon and held it up.

"What happened to your booze rules? There was a lot more in this a couple days ago."

"A rat got into it," Slater said.

Pike chuckled and swapped it for the scotch.

"You're no rat."

He poured them each a finger, and they tapped the glasses together.

"To the potential evolution of our narrative complex," Pike said.

Slater hoisted his glass. "To unlimited potential."

FOURTEEN

ALONE WHEN HE WOKE, Slater luxuriated in the warmth of the bed for a minute before he shoved aside the covers to face the cold air. His head felt clear—he must have stuck to his ration last night. He pulled on his skivvies and a T-shirt, and found Pike upstairs on the deck, in a sun lounger, working on his laptop.

Once Slater had poured himself a mug of coffee, he carried it outside.

"Aren't you cold out here?"

"It's a little chilly. But it's worth it." He set the laptop down. "You said your target was missing, but the police determined he left of his own free will."

"There's no law against that."

"There's also no indication that Lance is a knuck-lehead. The one thing that comes up is that the tax people want to talk to him. They think he owes Uncle Sam money on his crypto earnings. They issued him a two-million-dollar tax bill."

"So he's a damn gonif. If I owed them that much, I'd disappear too."

"They don't actually know how much he owes," Pike said, "or even if he owes anything. They just do that to get your attention. They'd do the same to you if you didn't file—make up a number and hang it out there." His eyes narrowed. "You do file, don't you?"

"My lawyer does it. At least I hope she does. I haven't had any stern letters or visits from the tax people, so I have to believe it's happening."

"I'm glad to hear you're totally on top of it."

Slater sat on the lounger, facing him, and set his cup on the ground. Leaning in, he ravished him, mouthing his neck and his jaw, running his fingers into his hair.

"You're giving me a stiffy," Pike said.

"We have to leave soon. That gives you a choice: food or sex."

"I can eat at the airport, but I can't get blown at the airport."

"Technically not true," Slater said, "but I like the way you think."

Shifting back, he unzipped Pike's pants and pulled out his cock, already chubby.

"Right here on the patio furniture?" Pike said.

"Just lie back."

Taking him into his mouth, Slater worked him, sensing the tension building in Pike's body. Pike groaned with pleasure, and finally strained into him as he came.

Still panting, he ruffled Slater's hair. "You're so freaking good at that."

"I wouldn't be if I hadn't slept with other people.

Just to provide some perspective on the new rules of our narrative complex."

Pike chuckled. "What do we do about you?"

Slater sat up and pulled out his cock, then moved closer, and squeezed it together with Pike's.

"Just look at me," he said.

He stroked himself against Pike, and Pike grasped his arm, and his thigh. Looking at him, and holding his gaze, Slater yelped as he climaxed, then sank on top of him.

"I don't think anyone ever got off just from looking at me before," Pike said, and caressed his back.

"I find that far-fetched," Slater said, pulling up. "You're extremely spank-worthy."

Grinning now, Pike was still breathing hard. That look in his eye. It was like he was lit up. Slater could hardly stand it. He put a palm on Pike's cheek, and leaned in to kiss his mouth, then rested his head on his chest.

Eventually it was time to leave, and they trooped down to the garage, and Slater drove them to LAX. As he pulled up to the curb in front of the terminal, Pike kissed him and then hauled his bag out of the backseat.

"See you in the ABQ in a few days," he said, leaning in the passenger door.

"I can't wait."

"Neither can my mother."

Slater chuckled. "I love that you're a mama's boy. You'd do anything for her."

"You only get one mother."

"She is a gem. Doris wants to meet her now."

Pike laughed. "I don't think we're there quite yet.

I love you, forty-niner."

"I love you too," Slater said, and felt a lump in his throat as he watched Pike drag his bag through the terminal doors.

His phone had buzzed a minute ago, when they'd been on the freeway, and he checked it now. It was a text from a number that wasn't in his contacts:

It's Desiree. We had kombucha on Tuesday. I have a job for you.

Tapping the number to call her, he set the phone in its mount and nosed into the traffic.

"What kind of job?" Slater said when she picked up.

"I need you to come to a meeting with me."

"You need somebody to protect you in case things get rough," he said. "In my business we call that babysitting. I don't do that."

"There's no danger. It's just to drop off a payment to an investor. I'm meeting him after dark, and it's a lot of money. As a woman it doesn't feel safe going alone."

"I still don't do that."

"I can pay you," Desiree said. "How much does your kind of babysitter earn? At least give me a ballpark number for what someone else would charge me."

"If it were me I'd need to get two grand, cash, up front."

"That's a lot," she said. "But I can swing it. I know you can handle the work. It's an easy two grand for you. Don't make me look for someone else."

Slater braked in the traffic and thought about it.

If she was willing to pay that inflated rate, he had to consider it.

"Is it for you personally or for the company?"

"Can we meet to discuss it?"

"I'm not driving out to the boonies again," Slater said. "I'll be in my office this afternoon. Bring the cash. And I'll warn you now—if there are any red flags, I'm not doing it."

Not waiting for a response, he ended the call, and merged onto the 105, and drove to his office. When he got upstairs the lights were on, and Max was at his desk, wearing his gray patterned suit, his necktie loose at his collar.

"How's your window-shade job?" Slater said, standing in his office doorway.

"Complicated." Max sat back. "I'm having trouble getting a money shot."

He meant evidence of the infidelity, Slater knew. Something that he could photograph.

"Are you sure it's really happening?"

"My gut says yes," Max said. "I might get an opportunity tonight. Surveillance and a tail. They actually live near here."

"Is Etta working with you?"

"I might get her to do a tail on the weekend if I'm still on this job."

"You know she's good at it."

He went into his own office, and once he got settled Max briefly stuck his head in to say good-bye on his way out. A knock came a while later, and he got up and pulled the front door open. Desiree. He opened it wider and waved her in. She was wearing a gray suit, cut to flatter her curves, with a necklace made of big metal loops. A slender briefcase dangled from one hand—she'd come here from work.

"This feels like a rough part of town," she said, following him into his office.

"It depends on what you mean by rough. It's a working part of town. Factories and wholesalers." He dropped into his desk chair. "Not everybody can work in suburbia selling imaginary money."

Desiree sat across from him, and set her bag on the floor, and frowned. "WeHo is not suburbia."

"From my vantage it is."

"Where do you live?"

"Here. In the city. With the rough people." Slater waved an arm. "Tell me what this meeting is about."

She shifted closer to the desk and held his gaze. "One of Wilma's investors wants to cash out. The Serbian. He's not a major player, so it's easy enough to pay him, but he's foreign, and he has security issues. We can't do an electronic transfer."

The intent eye contact, Slater thought. She was being so earnest. People sometimes did that when they were lying and really wanted him to buy in. But Desiree was corporate. Maybe she'd taken some communications seminar that taught the technique.

"So you're going to give him cash?" Slater said.

"Not quite." Reaching for her briefcase, she pulled out a sheet of paper and slid it across to him.

It was regular printer paper, with rows and columns of letters and numbers, grouped in even sets.

"This is random gobbledygook. A printout of a broken spreadsheet. It doesn't look like money to me."

"It is, though," Desiree said. "It's the key to a coin wallet. The wallet is worth about sixty million dollars."

"Not in actual money, I'm thinking," Slater said. "You're talking about Wilma's crypto product."

"The coin is money."

"Keep telling yourself that. Why not put this on a thumb drive? Or just email it to the guy?"

"Boris is neurotic," she said. "He insists it be completely disconnected from the cloud. From anything electronic. That way no one can hack him and steal it."

"How can he even verify that this is what you say it is without plugging it into a computer?"

"That's a Boris problem."

Slater stifled a scoff. "What's so dangerous about handing the guy a sheet of paper?"

"If people really are trying to steal from him, they might try to intercept me. Like when I show up where he's staying. I think Boris is paranoid, but maybe he has a reason to be. I just don't want to go alone."

"He doesn't live here?"

"Boris has the resources to drift around the world at his leisure. Right now he's staying in the Arts District."

"That's next to Skid Row, but it's not really a rough neighborhood," Slater said. "Not like here. It's where the hep cats go to groove."

"It's nearby, isn't it? It'll be a quick meeting."

"What does Boris do?"

"He's a rich guy who smears money around." Desiree waved a hand. "You know the type—Eurotrash. He invests in all sorts of things, apparently, including our company. Wilma calls him the Serbian. I don't know where his assets came from."

"And he doesn't want to invest in Wilma anymore?"

She shook her head. "He came to LA to cash out."

Slater tapped the sheet on his desktop. "Why doesn't he just go to your office to pick this up?"

"He's upset with Wilma right now. They're not talking. I'm the fixer, right, so I approached him privately, and he agreed to meet me and accept payment. He'll save face by not dealing with Wilma, and it'll get him out of our hair."

"Do you know if he carries a weapon? Does he have a bodyguard or a security detail? Are they armed?"

"I never saw anyone with him," Desiree said, "except paid escorts. They don't hang around for long. Otherwise he's always on his own. I've never seen a gun either."

"If it's really that simple, and nobody's going to be packing heat, sure—I'll hold your hand to go meet the Serbian."

"Excellent." She stood up. "I'll see you tonight."

"You have to pay me first."

"Can we do half now, half later?"

"No way, sister. This bus requires full fare up front."

Desiree frowned and dug in her briefcase. She produced a sheaf of bills and set them on his desk. "That should be it."

As she turned to walk out, Slater called after her. "Don't forget your expensive sheet of paper."

She paused in his office doorway. "Bring it with you tonight."

"You're going to leave something worth sixty

million dollars with someone you don't know?"

"I do know you." She gestured vaguely. "I know you enough, anyway. If you typed that into a computer, you wouldn't be able to do anything with it. Only Boris can. And maybe his enemies. None of them will be looking for you, but they might be looking for me."

He didn't protest as she walked out, and when he heard the front door close, he rose and locked it behind her. At his desk again he counted the cash she'd left. Two grand in C-notes. Squatting in front of the safe in the corner of his office, he dialed in the combination, and heaved it open, and put the bills inside. On the accounting envelope he added the date and a note:

Slater, babysitting, +2G

FIFTEEN

H EAVING HIS BOOTS UP on his desk, Slater pulled his keyboard into his lap and focused on the screen. The name Boris was too generic to find the right person, he knew, and even when he added "Serbian" to a query there were just too many people with that name.

Instead he dug for more details about Lance. Andy was his best bet for uncovering Lance's tracks online, but he wanted to read more about the guy, and soon got immersed in articles about the meteoric rise of his crypto product. Slater's attention was eventually pulled away by a knock at the door.

That was weird—it was still office hours, barely, but no one should be showing up here unannounced. Desiree wouldn't have come back. He locked his computer and got up, folding her cryptic sheet of paper in half a few times and tucking it into his hip pocket.

Treading out to the door, he opened it a few

inches to peer out. Brandon, the reality television guy, stood there, wearing chinos and a light leather jacket. He was with another man, a bottle blond, his roots intentionally left dark. His features looked Asian, and his snug trousers revealed an athletic body. The guy was basically fuckable, but that bushy haircut made Slater want to punch him in the face.

When he opened the door wider, Brandon beamed.

"You're really here."

"What are you doing here?" Slater demanded.

"I wanted to talk to you. This is my friend Oliver."

"Friend or boyfriend?" Slater said, looking him up and down.

"Mostly friend-friend," Oliver said.

"Oliver does video for the show."

"How did you find me?"

"I knew you weren't really a greensman," Brandon said. "Those guys never put out."

"Half the time they're women," Oliver said. "I bet they don't put out either."

Brandon raised his eyebrows. "And all those questions about Lance and Wilma. It didn't seem very on-brand."

"That's not an answer."

"Are you after Wilma's reward?"

"Might be."

"Can we come in?"

"Are you armed?" Slater said.

"You mean guns?" He frowned. "Of course not."

Oliver's tight little trousers weren't concealing anything, and Brandon didn't look to be packing either. Slater sighed, and stepped back, and waved them in.

"Cute," Brandon said, looking around. "I love deco. It's cozy."

He led them into his office and sat behind his desk. "I know it's small. We don't work on hundred-million-dollar budgets like your corporate masters do."

Oliver laughed. "Our budget is nothing like that."

Brandon sat across from him. "You don't have another chair?"

"You can grab the one from the front desk." He'd actually hoped they wouldn't be staying long enough to need to sit down, but he didn't say that.

Wheeling the desk chair in, Oliver dropped into it. "So what are your pronouns?"

"He and him," Slater said.

"I ask everyone. Just to be consistent. I don't want to make any assumptions."

"That's very considerate of you, and also very time-consuming," Slater said.

"That sounds like a microaggression."

His eyes narrowed. "Keep talking, and I'll gladly show you the macro version." He eyed Brandon. "Again, how did you track me down?"

Reaching for the plaster statue of Pollux with the horse, Brandon picked it up and looked it over. "Is this from anime?"

"Careful with that. His name is Pollux."

"It's written on the base. I haven't heard of this character. Is it Japanese?"

"Brandon—focus," Slater demanded.

He set the statue down. "Right. Where were we?"

"How did you find me?" he said, raising his voice.

"So, Oliver does video. He works on the show."

"You said that already," he shouted.

Oliver frowned. "Dude—chill."

"I asked him to send me a frame grab of your face from the dailies," Brandon said. "I searched for it on one of those facial recognition sites."

"There's a consumer version of that?" Slater said. "I thought it was only for the cops and the feds."

"I found a couple of sites, actually. It's a stalker's dream. It matches people from social media, the news, corporate websites."

"I'm not really on social media."

"But you do attract the attention of the authorities once in a while," Oliver said. "And you talked to a channel 6 reporter not long ago. Channel 6 is who runs our studio. I searched for your face in the in-house video archive."

"Your company uses facial recognition tech?"

"It's a different system, but yes, everything in the archive is catalogued. That clip was weird. It didn't have your name, but you were downtown somewhere, and you'd been attacked. You had blood all over your face. The software still made you."

"Damn it," Slater muttered. He was going to have to start wearing Svetlana's glasses.

"There's actually not that much about you on that facial database site," Brandon said, "but there was enough to get your name."

"Why were you filming me on the set?" Slater said. "I kept well out of the way."

"The cameras are rolling nonstop. You walked into frame a few times. It's inevitable." Oliver waved a hand. "Most people are happy when that happens. Maybe a director will notice you, and think you're photogenic, and put you in the script."

"What a freaking nightmare."

"You mean what an opportunity."

"Not everyone wants to be on television," Slater said.

Oliver's eyebrows shot up. "That's the stupidest thing I've ever heard."

"That's saying a lot, Oliver, considering you work in television." He eyed Brandon. "So you got my name from this facial recognition site?"

"Once I had your name, it was easy to find your office."

"So what do you want? You're hot, but the sex thing was just a one-time deal." Slater gestured to Oliver. "You've clearly got other options."

"It's not about that." Brandon's brow furrowed. "At first it was just curiosity. But then I saw you were an insurance investigator. I thought maybe you could help me. I keep getting in fender-benders."

"I don't work on car accidents."

He sat up. "These aren't accidents. Someone is orchestrating them. They're setting me up."

"Is it the same people who hit you?"

"Each time it's a different car, and a different driver."

"So what evidence is there that you're being set up?"

"It's happening to him so frequently," Oliver said, raising his eyebrows. "It has to be orchestrated."

He studied Brandon's face. "How old were you when you learned to drive?"

"What has that got to do with anything?"

"Answer the damn question."

He frowned. "I think I was twenty-two or twenty-three. I was a child actor, so I was pretty busy. All my schooling was with tutors."

"That explains it. If you don't learn before your brain solidifies in your late teens, you'll never be very good at it." Slater waved a hand. "You're just a bad driver."

Brandon scowled and spoke louder. "That's not it."

He raised his eyebrows and waited. He knew there'd be more.

"They're after me, Slater. I can't leave the house without my checkbook anymore. I know they'll break in and try to steal it."

"Who's they?"

"I have no idea. I want you to find out."

"What's the connection between the checkbook and the fender-benders?"

"It's complicated." Brandon huffed. "I haven't worked it all out yet. There's a lot going on. A lot of players. It has to be about extracting money from me, and degrading my credit rating. That's what makes the most sense."

"Who would hate you that much?"

"He's on a hit series," Oliver said. "The participants get hate posts online every day."

"People think I'm too ruthless on the show," Brandon said. "You saw the scene where I dumped Shawna."

"Did I? I just remember you and Shawna repeatedly accusing each other of having problems."

"That's what I'm talking about. I'm ruthless."

Slater frowned. "But it's not real. You're just playing a character."

"No one out there knows that."

He stifled a sigh and looked at Oliver. "Why are you here?"

"Moral support."

"You have to help me," Brandon said intently. "I won't take no for an answer."

"That's not how things work out here in actual reality. You're not going to put me on your sucker list."

Brandon scoffed. "I live in the real world."

"You live in reality TV. It's a different kind of real."

"So you're not going to help me."

Slater shook his head. "No way, brother."

"You suck," he spat.

"OK," Slater said, sitting up. "You nailed the delivery. Sharp and intense. But that kind of line only works on reality TV. That's not my framework. You can spare me your guff."

Brandon suddenly looked tired. "I don't have any other options here."

"Doesn't the studio have a security service? There's always guards hanging around those places. They'd know how to deal with your situation. You can't be the first celebrity to have a mysterious stalker."

Oliver sat up. "That's actually not a bad idea."

"You can even monetize it," Slater said. "Incorporate it into *Westside Reality Bros,* or do a one-off documentary, with the somber voice-over and the scary music."

"It's *Real Westside Reality Pros,*" Oliver said, and frowned. "How can you not remember that? You worked on the set."

"It's a brilliant idea," Brandon said. "I knew there

was a reason I had to come here. I can turn my personal anguish into content."

Slater watched him closely, not sure if he was being sarcastic. But from his expression he just looked relieved, even inspired, like he had a path forward now.

"I'll send you an invoice," Slater said.

"You're funny." Rising, Brandon adjusted his jacket. "Oh—there's another thing. You got me so horned up yesterday I couldn't think straight."

"That makes it sound like I assaulted you. You hit on me, remember? You're a damn dick-hound."

"Guilty," he said, and gestured dismissively. "You asked me whether Wilma would kill someone."

"Have you talked to her lately?" Slater said.

"That's not the point. You never asked me that about Lance."

"Do you think Lance could kill someone?"

He made his eyes wide before he spoke. It felt scripted, like he'd planned to do that. With actors it was probably safe to assume they were always acting.

"The guy is cold," Brandon said. "I mean, walking off with all that money. When we started in the industry, Wilma and I were the actors, the ones with the exquisitely refined people skills. Lance was just this weird computer guy."

"Did he ever act violently?"

"I saw him fly into a rage, screaming at people."

"Did he ever strike anyone," Slater said, "or threaten anyone?"

"Sure. Lots, back in the day."

"Back in the day?" Slater frowned. "You worked with them, like, what, a year and a half ago?"

"For me that's a lifetime ago. I'm not that person anymore."

"I guess your exquisitely refined people skills are still evolving. What kind of threats or violence did you see?"

"I remember he said to Wilma, 'I'm going to kill you.'"

"In what context?"

"In the office. They were arguing." Brandon shrugged. "If you go after him in Russia, just remember that he's dangerous."

Oliver rolled the chair back to the front desk, and Slater followed them to the door. As they stepped out, Oliver turned back.

"Groovy office, by the way."

Once he'd bolted the door behind them, Slater sat at his desk. Yet another character assessment of Lance, at least the fifth one he'd heard, and none of them aligned. It was no surprise that everybody was lying to him. But Brandon's version was no less likely to contain a kernel of truth just because he was a space cadet.

SIXTEEN

ON THE STREET DOWNSTAIRS Slater found a taco truck, and got a few bagged, and took them to his car. When he got home it was well after dark, and too cold to sit outside, so he ate at the dining table.

When it was time to go meet Desiree, he went down to the garage and pulled the sheet of paper out of his pants. Folding it open, he scanned the garbled jumble of letters and numbers. It was so hard to believe this was the key to that much dough.

Was he missing something? Desiree was probably lying to him, lying about some part of it, but he couldn't quite see the angle. It was odd that she'd left this with him. Maybe that was it—she was setting him up to get mugged, and he'd take the fall for the loss.

Folding up the sheet again, he pulled open the door of the Thunderbird, and flipped the driver's seat ahead, and climbed in the backseat. The molding at the top of the opera window on the side was easy to dislodge, and he pulled enough of it up that the edge of the fabric that covered the ceiling was exposed. It was tacked to the roof, but there were gaps, and Slater slid the folded paper inside. He pressed the molding into place around the window again, and felt the fabric. It was thick enough that it was impossible to tell there was something above it. No way would anyone find that paper, not without destroying his car first.

If everything went smoothly with Boris, it would be simple for Slater to step out and retrieve it. But if the plan was to mug him for it, to make him the fall guy, it would never be found.

Backing into the street, he waited for the garage door to roll down, then drove to his office. When he pulled into the parking lot across the street, it was mostly empty, but he spotted a black Tesla roadster parked along the fence. That had to be Desiree's car. He pulled up next to it and rolled down his window.

Desiree climbed out, still wearing her gray suit, and Slater reached across to push open his passenger door for her.

"I love your ride," she said as she climbed in.

"Why is it that tech industry people all drive the same car? For a while you were all in Priuses, and now it's those things." He backed up and then pulled into the street.

"You make me sound like a sheep. And crypto isn't really the tech industry."

"Of course not," Slater said. "You're disrupting things in a whole different way. Forging a new libertarian paradigm with breathtaking equal access for all. I probably wouldn't understand the nuances."

"Your words, not mine. Do you have the paper?"

"It's in my pocket."

"You folded it?" she demanded. "I hope it's still legible."

It was a short drive to the Arts District, and when he turned onto the narrow street she'd directed him to, Desiree pointed out the front of an art gallery.

"It looks closed," Slater said.

"Boris is renting an apartment upstairs."

He parked in front, and as they climbed out, he scanned the quiet street. Desiree was doing it too, he saw, her head swiveling as she glanced up and down the block.

"There's nobody around," he said.

The brick structure had probably been a warehouse or a small factory in its first incarnation, and he followed her up the exterior metal stairs at the side. Desiree knocked on the door, and a moment later a guy pulled it open.

In his fifties, maybe, he had a wiry blond brush cut, and stubble on his face, and sharp blue eyes. The track suit he was wearing was a little odd—bright green and made of something shiny, like silk or satin. The top was zipped down enough to reveal chest hair and several chunky strands of gold around his neck. Catching sight of Slater, he frowned.

"Who's this?"

"My assistant," Desiree said. "Are you going to let us in?"

"He doesn't look like an office worker," he said, and raised an eyebrow. "Are you armed?" His accent sounded a lot like Svetlana's.

Slater met his gaze. "I'm not."

His eyes flicked up and down Slater's form, then he whirled his finger in the air. "Can you do a little twirl?"

Later he'd remember that he should have taken that as a warning sign. It meant that this guy was no civilian, no leisure-oriented playboy. But Slater didn't react, and obediently did a three-sixty, and then followed Desiree inside. Boris wasn't armed either, he saw, looking him over. That shiny track suit was snug, and revealed a little paunch, but he didn't have a weapon under it. As he closed the door Slater caught a whiff of his cologne. That was a little Euro, but he was basically fuckable.

It was a sprawling room, the width of the whole building, with tall industrial windows over the street. It looked like a short-term rental, with no clutter, nothing personal on the walls. At one side was some lounge furniture, and farther back was a kitchen fronted by a bar with a trio of stools. Boris had music on, from a speaker over by the sofa, some upbeat classical piece, and he stepped over to turn down the volume.

"You have something for me?" Boris said as he came back.

"What's the hurry?" Desiree waved toward the bar. "Aren't you going to offer us a drink?"

Slater eyed her sidelong. That didn't fit with what she'd told him, that she was afraid of this guy, that this was supposed to be brief.

"Why not?" He threw up his hands and walked toward the bar.

They followed him over and watched as he took a bottle from a cupboard and set it on the bar top. It was scotch or bourbon, based on the color, but Slater didn't recognize the brand.

"I love your American whiskey," Boris said, and poured a shot into a tumbler, and handed it to Desiree, and then handed one to Slater.

"Not for me."

Boris gestured broadly. "You're going to insult me like this? You're in my place. You have to drink with me."

"Fine," Slater said flatly, and took the tumbler, and waited for Boris to pour his own. The three of them clinked glasses, and sipped, and Slater muttered, "Damn it."

"What's wrong with my alcohol?" Boris demanded.

"Nothing. That's the problem. I drink bourbon, but I've never had anything like this. I feel like I've been cheated." He eyed Desiree. "Like everything leading up to this has been a lie."

Boris laughed deeply. "I'm glad you like it." After he'd taken another swig, he turned to Desiree. "You owe me money."

"Technically it's the company that owes you money."

"I don't understand why we couldn't do this in your office," Boris said.

Desiree gestured to Slater. "Give the man the payment."

Before he could respond there was a loud *bang*. For a split second he thought the music had suddenly gone up in volume, a big bass drumbeat in the classical piece, but it had come from the wrong direction. Looking toward the source of the noise, he saw that the front door hung open now, and bodies were pouring in. Boris's eyes went dead, and he flashed his palms before anyone even said anything.

Two guys in jeans and black ballistic vests hustled into the middle of the room, pointing rifles at them. One of them shouted, "Hands, hands." Two more followed. Slater could feel his heart pound as he showed his palms. At least these weren't the people beefing with Boris. He could see the initials in white on the ballistic vests: ATF. These were feds.

One of them stood with his rifle pointed at them while another one, already wearing black latex gloves, stepped over and frisked each of them in turn. Slater knew the drill, and stood with his arms outstretched, his feet apart. This guy wasn't shy about groping his junk and checking between his legs. Eventually he called, "Clear."

Desiree looked wired, Slater decided, glancing at her. Her eyes were bright but she didn't look afraid. Boris just looked annoyed, like this was a waste of his time, the way people looked when the line got too long at the supermarket. One of the agents was breathing hard, he saw, his cheeks puffing out as he worked to dispel the adrenaline of busting in here. It made sense that they were amped up—if they came in armed, it meant they didn't know whether they were going to get shot at or not.

At the doorway a man and a woman in somber suits stepped in. They weren't wearing badges, but they had to be federal cops—the look was unmistakable. The guy was a little flabby, with dark Latin hair, and the woman was darker, her black hair pulled tightly back. As they walked over, Desiree spoke.

"You busted in too soon, you big dummy."

She gestured to Slater. "This is the one buying the Javelins."

"This guy?" the woman said, and frowned as she looked him over, and cocked her head.

"I knew I couldn't trust you," Boris snapped. "Wilma is a thief, and you are a thief. Damn you."

Desiree ignored him, her cool gaze on Slater. "He'll deny it, of course. But he has the payment on him."

The woman jutted her chin toward Boris, and the guy who'd frisked them stepped up and put a hand on his bicep, and pulled him away, steering him over by the sofa. They hadn't handcuffed him, Slater realized. That was curious. Regular cops would have everybody flat on the floor and hog-tied by now.

"What's your name?" the woman asked him.

"Slater Ibáñez."

At the entrance another guy in a suit stepped in, younger than the other two, maybe around thirty, with red hair and a bit of stubble. The cut of the suit flattered his body. Fuckable, Slater decided, even though he had the same bland cop vibe. He was gazing at a tablet, then looked up and called "Wilson."

The woman turned to him and raised her eyebrows.

"There's nobody downstairs," he said.

She jutted her chin at Slater. "Empty your pockets, cowboy."

"Are you the police department?" Slater said. "Don't you have to identify yourselves, or show your badges?"

She huffed and pulled out a black wallet, and folded it open, and flashed its contents at him. He caught a glimpse of her photo and the surname Wilson before she yanked it back.

"What did I just say?" she demanded.

Slater groaned and pulled out his phone, and his keys, and his cards, and his wad of cash, setting it all on the bar top.

Pulling on a pair of blue latex gloves, Wilson grabbed the cash and flipped through it. "There's less than two grand here."

"I know he has it on him," Desiree said. "Check under his shirt."

It had been a setup all along. Slater wanted nothing more than to go at her, but he forced himself to stand still and bite his tongue.

"Do you consent to a strip search?" Wilson said.

"If that will expedite things, sure," he said, and started to unbutton his shirt. Pulling it off, he tossed it on the bar, then crouched to untie his boots, and pulled each of them off. He stepped out of his jeans and his underpants, and set them next to his shirt, then peeled off his socks one at a time and tossed them on top. He was totally naked now, but no one seemed concerned. Resting his hands on his hips, he glared at Desiree.

Wilson picked up his jeans, feeling them carefully with her latex-clad fingers, even checking the seams. She ran his shirt through her hands, then picked up each of his boots, giving them a squeeze and looking inside, her nose wrinkling in disgust.

"He must have left it in his car," Desiree said, raising her voice. "Where's the payment, *cholo*?"

Slater gritted his teeth and avoided her gaze. Done pawing his clothes, Wilson rubbed her fingers together, studying them as if they were contaminated.

"Sir, where's your car?" she said.

"Right out front."

"Do you consent to a search of your vehicle?"

They were going to do it anyway, no matter what he said. Refusing them would only slow all this down.

"The keys are on the bar," Slater said. "Please go gently."

Grabbing the keys, Wilson tossed them to one of the black-vested guys. Wordlessly snagging them out of the air, he turned toward the door.

"It's the beautiful black Thunderbird," Slater called to him. "It's very sensitive."

Had he inadvertently left any of his surveillance gear in the trunk? Usually he only carried it when he needed it, for exactly this reason, the ever-present possibility of getting pulled over and searched. He'd put the tracker from Harold's Tacoma back on its charger, but he couldn't remember if there was anything else. If these chuckleheads figured out he had illicit tech, things would definitely go south fast.

Wilson scowled at him and waved a hand. "You can get dressed."

"Are you sure you're done?" Slater said, and raised his eyebrows. "If you have some lube, we can all take a look inside my colon."

Her lip curled in disgust, and she turned to Desiree. "You promised me, girlie."

"He had it when we walked in here," Desiree said, waving an arm. "You're the one who went and jumped the gun."

"This is not good. You let me down." Turning to one of the denim-clad agents, she gestured to the corner of the space, as far from Slater and Boris as possible. "Take her over there."

As Slater pulled on his shirt, he watched as the guy took hold of her arm. Desiree shrugged him away.

"Don't touch me," she snapped, and walked in front of him.

"How were you going to pay for them?" Wilson said, fixing Slater with that laser-beam cop glare.

"Pay for what?" he said, buttoning his shirt. "I didn't come here to buy anything. That crypto idiot hired me to protect her when she came to meet the Serbian. That's all I know."

"A crate of Javelins would set you back a lot of money."

Stepping into his jeans, Slater frowned at her. "I don't do track and field. I get plenty of exercise in the garden. Why would I buy sporting equipment from this guy? I never saw him before tonight." He tucked in his shirttails. "There's more of you police than there are of us. Are we being arrested?"

"That depends on what's in your car." She turned and stepped over to the corner where Desiree was.

Desiree stood with her arms folded, her expression a dark cloud. Over by the sofa, the flabby suited agent was engrossed in conversation with Boris. Both of them were talking calmly, but he couldn't hear them over the music.

The other suit, the redhead, stepped over to Slater as he pulled on his socks.

"Do you know an agent in Albuquerque named Pike?"

Slater jutted his chin. "Who's asking?"

He chuckled. "Pike's got a flag on you. He wants

to be copied on any and all contact."

"How did you ID me without actually looking at my ID?" Slater demanded.

The guy didn't answer, instead tapping at his tablet.

Looking over at one of the guys with the rifles, thankfully aimed at the floor now, he saw that he was wearing a body camera. It was subtle, a flat little box the same matte black as his vest, but that was his answer. Just like Svetlana had warned him.

"It's the body cameras," he said.

The redhead glanced up at him but didn't say anything.

"You ID'd me fast," Slater said, and stepped into his boots, and squatted to tie them, looking up at the guy. "That means it's an automated system. Do you look up every face the cameras pick up? You've got footage of my bare ass and my junk from multiple angles now too. Are you going to keep a record of that? Maybe your software could text me a reminder when it's time to trim my pubes."

The guy just laughed and walked away as Slater stood up. Watching Desiree and Wilson, he strained to hear their conversation, but he couldn't. Wilson definitely looked pissed. She crossed the room to Boris and the other agent, and the three of them spoke in low voices, their words obscured by the music.

A few minutes later the guy who'd taken his car keys came in. There was nothing in his hands—that seemed like a very good sign. He tossed the keys onto the bar.

"What did you find?" Wilson called to him.

"Lots of gardening tools, and a sledge hammer."

"That's a post maul," Slater said, loud enough for Wilson to hear him. "For pounding stakes. It's gardening equipment."

"No paper?" Wilson said.

"Just the registration card and gas receipts."

"No thumb drives, no electronics?"

"Nothing like that."

"Desiree," Wilson called to her. "Should we search his phone?"

"It's not going to be on his phone," she shouted. Even from across the room he could see the fury in her eyes.

Slater looked to Wilson. "That should do it for me, then. Am I still being detained?"

"Yes," she snapped. "So shut up until I say you can unshut it."

Wilson and the flabby suit stepped away from Boris, and stood with the redhead and the guys in denim near the front door. He wished he could hear what they were saying. Boris parked himself in the middle of the sofa, and stretched his arms out along its back, gazing at the dark sky outside the windows.

Finally Wilson spoke, loud enough for everyone to hear. "The uniforms can take Boryan. I'll debrief the informant."

"Way to blow my cover," Desiree said.

"You did that yourself when I walked in, girlie," Wilson said sharply. "Kevin, cuff the cowboy and take him to the office."

"You're arresting me?" Slater demanded.

"You're going to come in and make a statement."

"If that's all you need, I'll swing by in the morning."

"This can go one of two ways," Wilson said. "You come voluntarily now, or I detain you for the legally allowed maximum of forty-eight hours."

He huffed and folded his arms. That wasn't really a choice.

The redhead stepped toward him.

"You're Kevin?" Slater said.

"Correct."

"Why do you need to cuff me?"

He shrugged. "It's procedure."

"So let's get on with it. I've got stuff to do."

"We'll just wait for the boss to clear out."

"Is that also procedure?" He put his hands on his hips. "You seem to have an awful lot of those. Strip searches, handcuffs, breaking down doors. It's a lot of violence for people who dress like bank tellers."

Kevin met his gaze and spoke under his breath. "If you were smart, you'd shut your trap for half a minute."

Stepping over to the bar, Slater loaded his phone and his keys and his cash into his pockets, and they watched Wilson leave with Desiree, and then the guys in denim got Boris to stand up, and put handcuffs on him, and led him out too. Kevin waited a moment longer before he spoke.

"They should all be clear by now. Let's roll."

"I'm not getting cuffed?" Slater said.

"Even though you seem to be bent on pissing off Wilson, Pike says there's no need."

"You've been talking to him?" Slater demanded.

He chuckled. "Just texting."

"Damn it," Slater muttered, as he headed toward the door.

SEVENTEEN

N O ONE ELSE WAS outside on the dark street. Kevin pulled open the passenger door of a black Navigator that was parked behind the Thunderbird, then walked around to the driver's side.

"So how do you know Pike?" Kevin said, once they'd climbed in.

Slater scoffed. "Ask him, if you're so chummy."

"He just said he detained you on a terrorism investigation."

"That's true, but I wasn't the terrorist."

It was a short drive to the federal building, and Kevin waited on the ramp for the bomb-proof bollards to slowly retract into the ground, then drove into the underground garage. They boarded an elevator, and when they stepped off upstairs, it looked like a regular office, with an open-plan sea of desks that stretched to the dark windows along the wall. None of them were occupied at this hour. He wondered if this was the office that Pike had come to work in this week.

Kevin led him to a desk under the windows, and had him sit in front of it, then walked away. This was a lot more civilized than an interrogation room, he thought, looking around. He was being treated like a witness, not a perp. They must have bought his claim of ignorance. Or maybe it was Pike's influence. Wilson had said the meeting was about the sale of a crate of Javelin missile launchers. Those were tools of war. Of course the feds would be interested in that. Boris or whatever his name really was looked exactly like the kind of guy who'd be selling them, and Desiree had fingered Slater as the buyer. Just thinking about that smug look on her face made his blood boil.

When Kevin returned, he dropped into the desk chair. "I forgot to offer you a coffee, Mr. Ibáñez."

"I don't need coffee." Slater furrowed his brow. "Talking like that you make it sound like this is a bed-and-breakfast, not a police station. And call me Slater."

"We're not the police. But you already know that. I need to get your version of events."

"I don't have a version. I have the unalterable truth as I know it. Golden and constant and unwavering facts."

He grinned. "Lay it on me. Why were you there with Desiree tonight?"

"Aren't you going to record this?"

"I'm going to type up some notes," Kevin said, swiveling to his keyboard. "If I'm not looking at you, or responding to you, it doesn't mean I'm not listening. You have my full attention."

"OK, then." Slater explained what had happened today with Desiree—that she'd come to his office, and her story about needing a babysitter, and that she'd paid him. He omitted the part about the print-out she'd left on his desk.

"Did she tell you why she was going to see this person?" Kevin said.

"She just told me it was a business meeting."

"You weren't suspicious that they were conducting business at night, in a residence?"

"She'd just given me two grand. Cash has the power to wash away all the questions."

"When was the first time you met Desiree?"

"I was investigating someone in a child custody case," Slater said. "He was involved with her employer. The crypto outfit in West Hollywood. I met Desiree there, when I interviewed her about it earlier this week."

Kevin pounded away at his keyboard, and asked a few more questions, his eyes not moving from the screen. Watching him, Slater found the guy's red hair mesmerizing. Even the stubble on his jaw was electric orange.

"I know Desiree had something set up with your boss," Slater said. "Wilson called her the informant."

"I can't really discuss that."

"I wish I knew what the hell was going on," he said. "Who is this Boris guy? What did she want with him? What were you looking for in my clothes and in my car?"

When he finally stopped typing, Kevin met his gaze. "I guess it's not classified, and Pike says you're all right."

"So spill it."

"I've never heard him called Boris before. His real

name is Boryan. He's trouble, Slater. You don't want to be messing with him."

"Is he being charged with anything tonight?"

"Unfortunately we don't have a reason to. We found no evidence of any crime."

"Despite what Desiree promised you, it sounds like." That was probably bad news for Desiree, he realized, and for Wilma too.

Kevin sat back in his chair. "So how do you know Pike?"

"You're a persistent investigator, I'll give you that."

"He asked me what you were wearing. I told him you were buck naked for a while. He loved hearing that. I'm thinking there has to be a story there."

"It's more than a story, Kevin. It's a narrative complex."

"Pike actually said, 'Ibáñez is nothing but trouble, but he's mine.'"

"He said that?" Slater demanded.

"Does that resonate?"

Slater watched him for a moment. "I get it. You're just fishing." He sat up. "Am I free to go?"

"Of course." Kevin waved a hand. "We'll be in touch if we have any other questions."

"You could legit work in the hospitality industry," Slater said. "On the concierge desk at an upscale hotel."

"Uncle Sam pays a lot better, and concierges don't get to bust crooks."

"So is Desiree on ice tonight?"

"I can't really comment on that."

He got up, and Kevin walked with him through the sea of desks, back toward the elevators. When they passed a low fabric-lined divider, he saw Desiree, sitting in front of a desk like the one he'd just been at. Behind it was Wilson, reclining in her chair, her hands laced behind her head. Desiree looked up at him and scowled.

Stepping closer, Slater spoke intently. "You wanted to put me in the frame, you little grifter. You wanted to get me popped by the goddamn feds along with the Serbian." He jabbed a finger at her and shouted, "I'm not your fucking patsy."

Kevin grabbed his arm. "Come on, now."

"Where's the payment?" Desiree demanded.

"You keep saying that," Slater said. "I don't know what you're talking about. You should stop listening to the voices in your head. Take your medication."

"Get him out of here," Wilson snapped.

Slater let Kevin pull him away, but he called back to her over his shoulder. "I wouldn't want to be you tonight, toots. Boryan is on the streets."

In the elevator lobby Kevin pressed the DOWN button and furrowed his brow. "Why would you do that?"

"She tried to get me busted," Slater said. "If there weren't a bunch of cops around it would have gone a lot worse for her."

"I don't need to hear that," he said, and stepped onto the elevator.

"How do I get back to my wheels? Am I hoofing it?"

"I can take you."

On the ride down, Slater eyed him sidelong. Kevin had his hands in his pockets, displacing his jacket enough to reveal the compelling shape of his glutes. In the garage they climbed into the Navigator again. The Arts District wasn't far from here, he realized. He could have just walked.

"You're in good shape," Kevin said, nosing the vehicle up the ramp and onto the street. "Do you work out?"

"I wish I could say the same about you, but I was the only one who had to do the burlesque tonight."

He laughed. "In case you missed it, that was a pickup line."

"You're a total smoke show, Kevin, and the red hair thing just augments it. But I can't do it."

"You like redheads?"

"In my experience, red means stop."

"That sounds like a stereotype."

"In different circumstances I'd be all over you," Slater said. "Who wouldn't be? You're buff and they let you carry a gun. But my life is way too complicated right now."

"I get it. You're committed to Pike."

That had to be a guess, Slater decided. No way would Pike have told him that. They rode in silence for a while, then Slater spoke.

"Did Pike tell you to hit on me?"

"What? No, that's all me. Why would he do that?"

"Did anyone ever tell you that cops and robbers don't mix?"

"Personally I find that particular combination pretty damn steamy," Kevin said.

Back in front of the shuttered gallery, Kevin pulled up behind the Thunderbird, and Slater climbed out.

"Five stars for door-to-door service," he said, leaning in to meet his gaze.

Kevin laughed. "Get some sleep."

He closed the door and watched the Navigator pull away, then opened the trunk of the Thunderbird. His tools had been moved around, with some of them spilled out of their duffel bag, and they'd pulled up the carpet, and even lifted the spare without bothering to bolt it down again.

"Idiots," he muttered.

But nothing was missing. He spent a minute stowing the tools, and shifting the tire back into place, and twisting the wing nut onto the plate that held it down. Once he'd slammed the trunk he got in behind the wheel and looked around. Had they bugged his car? Probably not—they didn't seem that well organized, and they'd need permission first. All those rules and procedures. They couldn't just do it on the fly like he could.

Digging out his phone, he dialed Andy.

"It's late," he said when he picked up.

"This is business," Slater said, "and it's kind of urgent. Can I come by?"

"Can you tell me on the phone?"

"I need to show you something."

Andy sighed. "I really want to … say no."

"That means yes," Slater said. "I'll be there soon."

He ended the call, and drove to Broadway, and pulled in behind Andy's building. The lot was crowded at this hour, with all the bars and clubs around, and the attendant was still on duty. Climbing out, he went over and paid the guy, then walked back to the Thunderbird and leaned on it for a minute, arms folded, scanning the lot and the street beyond. He wanted to make sure he wasn't being tailed, wasn't being observed.

A group of pedestrians walked by, boisterous and not even glancing in his direction, and none of the passing vehicles slowed down. He opened the car door again, and pulled the seat ahead, and climbed into the back. Working in the dark, he retrieved the folded-up sheet of paper from under the ceiling fabric, then pressed the molding back into place. He tucked the paper into his hip pocket and climbed out.

When he knocked, Andy pulled his door open, clad in a T-shirt and boxers.

"I was already in my PJs," Andy said.

"You're always in your damn PJs."

He chuckled and led him inside. The computer screens were lit up, and he had the radio on.

"You were totally still working," Slater said.

Andy sat at his desk and swiveled toward him. "What have you got that's so important?"

"I got detained by the feds tonight because of this." He pulled out the sheet and folded it open. "I need to know what it is."

He looked it over, his lack of fine motor control making the paper tremble in his hand. "It might be a key for something that's ... encrypted. Why would you print it out?"

Slater pulled a chair over from the table, and sat, and explained what Desiree had told him about it.

"If you scan that and use it online," Slater said, "will the Serbian know? I don't want anyone coming after you."

"I can avoid leaving tracks. The only way to ... find out if it's legit and what it's for is to reassemble it."

He flashed his palms. "Then go for it."

Andy ran it through his scanner, then spent a minute with a text editor. At first Slater watched him work, but then shifted his attention to his phone. Eventually Andy swiveled toward him.

"Your contact implied that it was … a private key," Andy said. "It's not that. It's the whole key. The public … part and the private part. Full access. It's for a … wallet with Wilma's flavor of crypto in it."

"Can you see what it's worth?"

"I can assure you it was never worth sixty … million bucks. It might have been worth six million before … the last crash. Right now it's more like … six hundred bucks."

"Does Desiree know that?"

"Of course she does. She printed it out."

"What about the Serbian?"

"If he knows the wallet's address, he can see … what it's worth without this. You only need the … key if you want to access it."

"I bet Boryan never got specifics," Slater said. "Desiree was playing him too. They never intended to give him anything. And nobody's going to come after me for six hundred bucks."

"A homeless junkie might."

Slater sat back. "I bet there's not many of them who dabble in crypto."

Swiveling his chair, Andy pulled the sheet out of his scanner and offered it to him.

"Why don't you keep that?" Slater said. "Can it be payment for this?"

"I suppose I could play with it. It's really more work to … sell it than it's worth." He set the sheet aside. "I'm making some progress on Lance. I might have … something for you by tomorrow."

"Let me know," he said. "Do you have time to mess around?"

"No," Andy said firmly. "Where's your out-of-towner?"

"He's out of town."

"Not my problem. You have to go."

Slater rose and leaned in to kiss him. "Bye, beautiful."

Walking around to his car, he could feel the tension leaving his body, his muscles relaxing. That sheet of paper was meaningless. He knew that now.

At his house, once the garage door had rolled down, he climbed the stairs and pulled his fifth of bourbon out of the pantry cupboard. Once he'd poured a couple of fingers into a tumbler he took that first satisfying sip. It would never be as good as that stuff Boryan had. Of course there was always going to be something better, but he wished he'd never tasted that.

The buzz of his phone interrupted his thoughts. It was Pike. Slater flicked off the lights as he answered, and carried his tumbler over to the sofa, and sat in the dark.

"Hey, Reddy Kilowatt. Zap."

"You certainly had an interesting evening," Pike said.

"And you already know all about it. Why do you have a flag on me?"

"Because I care about you. So that maybe I'll have the chance to intercede if you get into trouble. It sounds like you're dancing awfully close to that. I'm gone for twelve hours and you wind up in the middle of a sting operation."

"I can take care of myself."

"Boryan is bad news," Pike said. "We've been after him for years."

"He's an arms dealer?"

"That's not illegal. He's an arms smuggler, allegedly, and that makes him interesting to us. How the hell did you get tangled up with him?"

"I told you about Lance and Wilma. Apparently Wilma owes him money." Slater took a sip, then set his tumbler on the carpet, and stretched out. "Kevin probably told you most of it already. I think he figured out that we're together, by the way, if that matters."

"I never told him that."

"You asked him what I was wearing."

Pike laughed. "That was to provide context."

"Well, he hit on me after. I didn't go home with him because I'm actually capable of self-restraint. Even when you're not around. You're welcome."

EIGHTEEN

S LATER WOKE TO THE buzz of his phone on the bedside table. It took him a minute to swim up to consciousness, and when he grabbed it, he saw that it was late. He'd slept hard after the adrenaline rush of people pointing rifles at him, and getting strip-searched, and a brush with the federal hoosegow. It was a text from Andy:

I've got something. You can stop by.

Such a little prick, gatekeeping him like this. Granting him permission to visit. Like if he showed up unannounced it would disrupt his workday, or he'd trash the place, or stuff would go missing. But it sounded like he'd found details about Lance.

Once he'd made himself some coffee, he went back to his bedroom to get dressed. Yesterday's jeans were still presentable, and he pulled on a dark collared shirt, then hustled down to his garage and drove downtown.

When Andy pulled the door open, he followed him inside and found Kyle on Andy's bed, propped up on the pillows, gazing at his phone. Buff and with great dark hair, Kyle was wearing chinos and an expensive-looking sweater.

"What's he doing here?" Slater demanded. He looked to Kyle. "Are you OK there, cupcake? I could get you a few more mattresses if you're experiencing any discomfort. There might be a pea under that one."

Kyle scowled at him. "You look a little wound up. Have you taken your amoxicillin today? You're supposed to abstain from sex for a while when you've got the STDs. I guess more than a few hours would be a challenge for you."

"Like I'm going to take grown-up advice from the first delicate blossom of spring," Slater said. "Why are you wearing trousers anyway? I know your mom hasn't actually graduated you from knee pants yet."

"Booze hag," he said intently.

"Scum," Slater said through his teeth.

From his desk, Andy shouted at them. "Knock it off, both of you. Slater, grab a chair."

Pulling one from the table, he sat next to Andy's desk chair, positioning it so that he could keep an eye on Kyle in his periphery. Andy swiveled to face him.

"I think I found evidence of … Lance doing stuff online. I'm not totally sure. It might … be a bit of a leap."

"Explain it to me," Slater said.

"First, I looked at the money. Lance didn't keep … his half of the coin. The company owned over eighty percent … of the total in-house. Forty-one percent was … traded rapidly just before the third big crypto crash, in thousands of … individual transactions. That was also just before Lance … evaporated. It was him cashing out."

"Someone else said that—the third crash. How many crashes have there been?"

"A few," Andy said. "The one they call the third was … the worst. It wiped out a lot of value across the sector. Dozens of prominent … coins were obliterated for good."

"Are you sure all that trading was Lance converting it to cash?"

"I'm no forensic accountant, but selling and buying … activity is posted publicly. Anything run with … blockchain is public by design. It sure looks like someone was after real money."

"Does that point us to where he is now?"

"Not directly. There are web forums … about crypto, with lots of back-and-forth about Lance and … Wilma's coin. Mostly it's sore losers who got cleaned out."

"If crypto is a grift," Slater said, "of course there's going to be lots of victims."

"I read through all the people trash-talking Wilma's … company. Everyone calls her a chiseler, except the ones who are obvious … company plants. But several of the critics had the tone of people who knew more than … ordinary investors would have."

"Insiders."

Andy raised his eyebrows. "That seems likely. Digging into those users, it turns out a whole lot … of them are using the same anonymizing server."

"What does that mean?"

"It implies they were all the same … person.

Lance fits the profile of an insider."

"That sounds like a great lead."

"If it's him. Maybe there are other pissed-off … former employees." He waved a hand. "People are too reliant on … anonymizers. They don't expect that they can be traced."

"But you did it."

"Kind of. When you aggregate the activity of … all these users, there's enough information to trace them farther. It turns out … they were all using the same satellite internet provider."

"So they are the same person," Slater said.

"That's pretty damn likely. A preponderance of … evidence, as the lawyers say. But that still doesn't … prove that it's Lance."

Kyle got off the bed and slung a backpack onto his shoulder. "If you two are playing spies, I'm going to the gym."

"We're not playing, son," Slater said. "This is the real world. People without trust funds."

He scoffed and walked out.

"If you weren't so into him," Slater said, "I'd punch that guy in the face."

"You need to find a way to … tolerate him. He's not going away."

That was a dark thought, but Slater waved dismissively. "Internet providers have to keep track of where their users are, right? Can you get an address?"

"I couldn't get into their records using … traditional techniques."

He meant breaking in, Slater knew. "So what's the next step?"

"There are other data sets. The provider is quite …

proud of their constellation of satellites, and they've … made public a lot of information about them. I was able to find out where the satellites were when that cluster … of users was connected. It was always in the same area. That means he's not … moving around."

Swiveling to his computer, Andy pulled on his black plastic gauntlets. They were an input device that compensated for his lack of fine motor control. On the screen he pulled up an image with dozens of purple lines running across it. They formed a cross-hatch pattern, with half running lower left to upper right, and the rest at right angles to them.

"These are the paths of the satellites during the time they were … connected to his computer," Andy said.

Slater leaned closer, studying the screen. "This is amazing. Why are there some at different angles to the rest?"

"Those are satellites in a higher … shell. There are fewer of them. They're in different orbits."

"Where is this, and how much territory does it cover?"

"Let me zoom out, and turn on the base layer."

Under the purple lines a map appeared. It was a big chunk of the West, Slater saw. As Andy zoomed out, the end points of each satellite track came into view. Overall they formed a vague oval, lengthwise spanning Baja to Idaho, and east-west from San Fran to Salt Lake.

"It's interesting," Slater said, "but not very informative. There must be fifty million people living under those tracks."

"The user's antenna isn't just anywhere inside …

that oval. It has to be near the focal point." He zoomed in on the map, and a green circle appeared, encompassing a wide swath of California.

"Landers," Slater said, reading the label near the middle of the circle. "I know where that is. Out in the Mojave."

"The problem is that I can't calculate … the focal point exactly. This circle is the area where the antenna could be. It still covers … a lot of land."

"It's pretty nonspecific."

"You can narrow it down more though," Andy said. "About forty percent of the area of the circle is … on the military base. See this line? He can't be … in there. It's a bombing range."

"Even outside the base, that circle must cover ten thousand houses."

"My estimate is about eight hundred individual structures or … groupings of structures."

Slater chuckled. "You're so good at this. A skip-tracing minx."

"I'm glad to hear you say that, because unfortunately it's … going to cost you more this time. I had to pay some … gratuities."

"We'll get to that. If this user has satellite internet, they have to be connected to the electric grid. Does that eliminate any of the structures?"

"There's lots of abandoned homesteads." He zoomed in on a collection of buildings. "That's an electric pole. You can trace where the line goes by … finding the next pole, but you can't see the wires."

"So it might be disconnected, but you'd never know."

"Even abandoned properties might … still have

the wires connected. This will tell you which places aren't near a … power line, though. Those are definitely not on the grid."

"Any ideas on how to narrow down the possibilities?"

"The green circle contains the … focal point, and the highest probability is that the user is … in the center of that. You could focus on a five-mile radius right in the middle and they'd … almost certainly be within it. You can also get much better … satellite photos of the ground, but you have to pay for them."

"How much?"

"It's business-level pricing, so probably a couple … grand. I'll send you the details for the vendors. They'll ask you why … you need the images. Just make something up. Something that sounds … legit, like you're counting cacti for … your thesis or something."

"This is such great work," Slater said. "What do I owe you?"

"You can't get pissed at me."

"I know you said there were payoffs."

"It was also a lot more work than … normal. I stayed up half the night after you left."

Slater gestured impatiently.

"Fifteen hundred."

"Damn it," he snapped. "That's really pushing it."

"I got results for you. Focus on that."

"Can we deduct the six hundred in crypto?"

"You know damn well that's not worth anything."

Rising and digging out his wad, Slater had just enough cash, and handed over the C-notes.

"You cleaned me out, chiseler."

"If you collect that reward for Lance," Andy said, "this will be a drop in the bucket."

"You saw that, huh." He leaned in to kiss him. "Bye, beautiful."

———·———

AT SLATER'S OFFICE THERE were still some day laborers hanging around the lobby, and upstairs the lights were off. At his desk he looked through everything Andy had sent, then sat back to think about it.

Was looking for Lance pointless now? If Wilma was too broke to pay her investors, there wouldn't be any dough to pay anyone that reward. Even if she managed to acquire Lance's fabled assets, she'd just stiffed Boryan, a much scarier guy than Slater. Why wouldn't she pull the same thing with him?

He'd just spent a lot of dough on Andy's research. Sunk costs weren't a good enough reason to push ahead with the quest, he knew that. But it felt like a moving train, like something he had to see through. Maybe he'd give up if there weren't any likely target properties to investigate. At least he had to look through all this.

The publicly available satellite images of that part of the Mojave just weren't detailed enough to get a good sense of whether the homesteads were occupied or not. Looking at the website of one of the satellite imagery providers, Andy's price guesstimate had been accurate. It was expensive, but it was the only way—he had to shell out for the more detailed images. Unlike the public ones, these had been taken recently, which might help.

The site was all self-serve, and besides payment,

he had to provide a corporate tax identity. That was easy enough, as he and Max had that set up. In the pull-down menu for "intended use," there were only a dozen options, so he chose "mineral prospecting."

The images were available as soon as he'd paid, and he got into it, poring over the detailed overhead photos of the endless desert landscape. There were a lot more homesteads than he'd thought would be there, and there were a startling number of junkyards. Mostly they were agglomerations of wrecked cars, but some also had stacks of pallets, and piles of tires, and what looked like lengths of pipe. The resolution of these photos was high enough that he could see the individual vehicles and the black ring shapes of the old tires.

Some of the places didn't have electricity, with no lines running nearby, which meant he could eliminate them as possibilities. Sitting back in his chair, he thought about it. Maybe that wasn't the way to sort through them. Like Andy said, he should start at the most likely point, the very center of the circle.

From Andy's map it was hard to pinpoint the center exactly, but he picked a spot and zoomed in on the general neighborhood in the high-resolution images. The dirt double-track roads and developed land stopped abruptly at the boundary of the military base, and that clear demarcation ran through his estimated center. Near that point, right on the edge of the base, was a homestead with no evident house, just a few small flat-roofed structures and a dozen cars. There were no electric lines to the property, so this wasn't a candidate. But then something caught his eye—evenly spaced black bars, lined up east-west, positioned next to one of the structures. Zooming closer, he could see the glint of sunlight on black glass. Solar panels. He'd made a stupid assumption—not being wired to the grid didn't mean there was no electricity.

Looking at the rest of the property, it didn't make sense—the small shacks and wrecked cars, and then the modern solar array. Why would you install fifty grand worth of solar and not upgrade the structures? The tidy gray rectangle near the panels might be the storage battery for after dark. There was a round white object on the opposite side of the structures, just a few feet across. He'd seen those before in the countryside. A water well. That was the dome-shaped housing for the pump. This place looked rough at first but it had self-contained juice and running water—it was totally off the grid.

Someone was living there. If it were abandoned, they would have sold off the solar installation. Looking at the county map, the property was large for the area, described as "242.3 acres." It was zoned as rural, although no agriculture was going on there— the land hadn't been cleared of the native plant life, except right around the structures, and there were no animal pens. The owner was listed as someone named W. Goff, and he'd bought the place sometime the year before last.

This was a tantalizing possibility. It was near the center of Andy's antenna circle, and the building site was far from the property line, right back against the wilderness of the military base. Nobody could see what Goff was up to.

He had to go out there, he knew that now. Reward

or not, it was too compelling not to. But it was a long drive—if it wasn't Lance's hideout, he needed backup places to check out. Hunched over his desk, he pored over the satellite photos, working his way outward from the center of the circle. Eventually he'd marked a dozen other possibilities, numbering them in order, with the most likely candidates first. That was probably as many as he could get to in a single day. And none of them looked as solid as the Goff place.

NINETEEN

OZING, HIS CHIN ON his chest, Slater started awake when he heard the sound of the door handle. Locking his computer with a keystroke, he sat up and waited, listening. Max or Etta would use their keys next. No one else should be trying to walk in, even on a weekday afternoon.

A sharp knock came, and he got up to pull the door open a few inches, his boot planted firmly inside it. Wilma stood there, wearing a black turtleneck and jeans.

"What do you need, sister?"

"To talk. Can I come in?"

"Is this about last night? You should be talking to Boryan. I bet he wants to talk to you."

"Are you seriously going to make me stand in the hallway?"

He stifled a sigh and pulled the door open. Behind her was a man—tall and bulky, with a shaved head and a busted nose. His tweed jacket didn't hide the fact that he was a bodyguard, or a bouncer, or the heavy. Under his arm was the telltale bulge of a weapon.

"Who's your boyfriend?" Slater said, blocking the doorway. "Why is he armed?"

"Don't worry about Carl," Wilma said. "I thought you were going to let us in."

"Not with the armed gorilla."

"I just want to talk."

Slater sighed. "With friends like Boryan, I guess you'd need a bodyguard." He eyed Carl. "No monkey business."

They followed him into his office and faced the desk as Slater dropped into his chair. Carl stood with his feet apart and folded his hands over his belt buckle, the way cops and military people did. Conrad called it the fig-leaf stance. In a way it projected authority, but from this goon it just made Slater want to punch him in the face.

"This place is tiny," Wilma said.

"I don't have investors to impress the way you do," Slater said. "High-tone people like Boryan. Why don't you sit down? That's what the chair is for."

Wilma ignored that. "What exactly have you found out about Lance?"

"Since Monday?" he demanded. "What you've told me, and what was in the media after he disappeared."

"I know you've been talking to other people who worked for me."

"Of course I have. It's called research."

"So what else have you turned up?"

"I'm just getting started," Slater said. "And I'm definitely not going to share anything with you now—you'll try to cut me out of that hot million. Is that really why you're here? I know Desiree didn't cook up that frame job on her own. Boryan doesn't seem like the kind of guy who'll forgive and forget. If I were you I'd watch my back."

"About that," Wilma said. "You have something that belongs to me. A sheet of paper. I need you to return it."

"We both know that paper is worth next to nothing. Besides, I can't believe you'd print it and not keep a copy of it on your computer. The printout was just a prop for the feds. You want it back because it's evidence of what you were trying to pull. If Boryan got hold of it now, he'd have proof that you were scamming him."

She glanced at her companion. "Carl."

Carl reached into his jacket, and drew his handgun, and leveled it at Slater. "Keep your hands where I can see them."

"Don't point your gun at me," Slater snapped.

"You're not the one giving orders," Wilma said. "Tell me where that sheet is."

"I can't believe you'd try to strongarm me in my own office. Is that a Five-Seven? You know they armed the Nazis, right? What is wrong with you?" Slater demanded.

"Look at me," Wilma said. "I asked you a question."

"Did you not notice the camera in the lobby, or the camera in my front office? If you pop me, even an incompetent police detective would take five minutes to go through my case notes and match your name to the video." He gestured at Carl, then at Wilma. "The armed gorilla and the poseur who's dressed all

Silicon Valley."

"There's no cameras," Carl said. "I checked."

"Answer the question," Wilma shouted.

"So what," Slater said, "if I don't squawk, you're going to plug me, and bury me in the Angeles National Forest next to Lance?"

"I didn't kill Lance, you moron. I'm trying to track him down."

He raised his eyebrows. "That's not what I heard."

"Who told you I killed him?"

"I can't really reveal my sources."

Keys rattled in the front door.

"Who's that?" Wilma demanded.

"My business partner. The other name on the door." Eyeing Carl, he added, "Don't cap him. I'll get rid of him. Just shut up and let me talk."

Carl waggled his weapon and stepped sideways so that his bulky frame was blocking the office doorway. "Don't try anything," he said, "or you both get lead supplements."

"Hey, Max," Slater called. "I'm just cooking some pigeons. Do you need the office?"

"Don't mind me," Max called back. "I'll be out of here in a second. I forgot some paperwork."

Slater eyed Wilma and held up a finger, urging her to keep quiet a moment longer. Max had definitely understood what he meant by "cooking pigeons"— it was one of their mutually agreed distress signals. The guy never came in to pick up paperwork. That all stayed in neglected piles on his desk.

The sound of a drawer opening and closing came from his office, and Max whistled a tune. He never did that either. It was to let Slater know he'd received the message.

"Cooking pigeons?" Wilma said quietly.

"It just means interviewing clients."

Carl glanced sidelong, shifting his head to see the front office in his periphery, but he didn't turn away from Slater, and the muzzle of his weapon never wavered.

"Where did you get that suit, Carl?" Slater said, trying to draw his attention. "In the Dumpster behind a homeless shelter?"

Then came the sound of a meaty *thunk*, and Carl's eyes rolled up, and he collapsed, his shoulder striking the corner of Slater's desk before he slumped to the floor.

"Oh," Wilma cried, and put a hand over her mouth.

Max was standing in the office doorway, in his dark-red suit, a collapsible steel baton in one hand and his pistol in the other. He aimed it at Wilma.

"Reach for the sky, San Jose."

Wilma's eyes were wide, and she flashed her palms as she took a step back.

"Yeah," Slater shouted. "Your timing is impeccable, partner. I want to kiss you right now."

"No thanks," Max said, and to Wilma, "Are you armed?"

"What? No."

Slater grabbed a pair of black latex gloves from his bottom desk drawer and snapped them on as he stood up.

"What's going on here?" Max said.

"These idiots have no manners." He scooped up Carl's handgun.

"Is that a Five-Seven?"

"I know, right?" Slater briefly popped out the magazine, then snapped it back in. "Full mag. This chump thinks he's a cartel boss."

"What did you do to him?" Wilma said.

"He won't be out for long."

Squatting, still aiming his weapon at Wilma, Max tapped the end of the asp on the floor, collapsing the concentric extensions into a black cylinder the size of a pocket flashlight.

"What is that thing?" Wilma said.

"What thing?" Max tucked it into his jacket pocket. "I don't know what you're talking about."

On the floor Carl groaned and rolled onto his side.

Slater jutted his chin at Wilma. "It's pretty freaking nervy to come in here and draw down on me. You must be desperate."

"I need that document."

"Bullshit. Why would you come here and do this? It tells me there's a time constraint. Is Boryan about to drop the hammer? Are you in hock to the Slovenians or the Slovakians too? Is your house of cards on the verge of collapse?"

Carl was lucid now, and looked up at him. "That's mine."

Pulling the slide back, Slater screwed one eye shut and aimed the weapon at his head, then lifted it and let the mechanism pop back into place.

"Not anymore, chum. I get why the Germans liked these. It's really lightweight."

He sat up on one elbow. "Give me that."

Slater kicked him in the gut. "That's for pulling a gun on me."

Groaning, Carl pulled his knees up into a fetal ball. Slater kicked him in the ribs.

"That's for threatening to ventilate my partner." He kicked again, eliciting a shrill yelp. "Why do you make me do this to you?"

"Enough," Max said, raising his voice. "He gets it. Cops or no cops?"

"There's no need to call the police," Wilma said quickly. "I'll admit that things got a little out of hand. Carl felt threatened."

"Fuck you, you lying dirtbag," Slater said. "Your tech-bro rules don't work here." He eyed Max. "No cops."

"What about her?"

Slater pointedly looked Wilma up and down. "Maybe I'll plug her with the Five-Seven." He waggled the weapon. "It has this dipshit's prints on it. I'll turn it in anonymously. I just have to grab a shovel and find a nice quiet spot in the mountains."

"That's absurd," Wilma said, her eyes wide. "Why would you do that? The reward is still on the table. It won't be if I disappear."

"Four rounds," Slater said, eyeing Max. "Two in the head for each of them. Do you think the neighbors would hear that?"

"It's late in the day," Max said, his brow furrowing. "Lots of people in the building are already gone. Rosario works late. I'll go up the hall and flirt with her and tell her somebody knocked a sewing machine onto the floor. That would account for the noise. She'll tell everybody that."

"There's no need for this," Wilma said, raising her voice. "Let's just talk this through."

"You're the one who brought the rod." Slater squinted and aimed it at her head for a moment before he dropped his arm. "What do you think, partner?"

"I don't know if it's worth the effort," Max said. "There's just so much trash. Are you going to try to bury it all? This gorilla looks heavy too. Hauling him out of here won't do my sciatica any favors."

At their feet Carl was still curled in on himself, his breathing raspy.

"I have a tarp in my car," Slater said, "and I know that guy on the sixth floor would loan us his platform truck. It fits in the elevator."

"Still, think about the digging part. That'll take up most of your evening. Plus an hour in the car up to the mountains, and an hour back. There's nowhere to eat up there. We'd have to take snacks."

"How about this," Slater said, turning to Wilma. "You're going to let go of that printout. I'm not going to give it to Boryan because I'm not interested in getting mixed up in your bullshit racket. Losing it is the cost of trying to set me up as your fall guy."

"That was Desiree's idea."

"It doesn't matter," he said, raising his voice. "I'm going to continue looking for Lance, and if I find him, you're going to pay me. Big time. All six zeroes."

"Of course," she said quickly, nodding her head.

"If you send your apes after me again, I'll come by your place and smash up the zoo."

"I get it, Slater. You don't know where Lance is yet."

"If I ever see this asshole again, I'll do a lot worse than sap him."

"Carl," Wilma said. "Catch yourself. We're leaving."

He slowly got to his feet, and massaged his bicep, and fixed Slater with a murderous glare. Slater waggled the handgun.

"You can pick this up at the police station. The one on First. For your sake I hope there's no ballistics records on it, because your prints and DNA are all over it."

Max backed into the front office and gestured with his weapon. "Out. Both of you." Once they'd trudged into the hall, he bolted the door behind them, and lifted his jacket to holster his weapon. "You meet the nicest people in this job."

Slater chuckled. "Thanks, buddy. You saved my neck."

"That sucker should have been watching me, not you. He thought he was safe because I couldn't see his weapon."

"It's my own damn fault. I saw that he was armed and I let them in anyway. I figured I knew her already, and things had been civil, that she just wanted to talk. But that was really stupid. My romantic narrative complex is distracting me. Making me soft."

"You can't blame it on love. Did they come here to grease you?"

"It was just a threat. To coerce me into talking." Slater held up the Five-Seven. "What do I do with this?"

"You know some cops. Give it to them. Or break it up and trash it."

"I can't really risk being stopped with this, even if it's in pieces."

"I'll handle it," Max said, and reached for it. "If you're not turning it in, why did you put the gloves on?"

"So that Wilma would believe I was actually thinking about using it on her."

"I get it. The goon probably bought that you were going to give it to the cops too."

"I hope he won't come back here looking for it."

"He won't," Max said. "I'll dismantle it and drop the parts in a couple of storm drains. The mag I'll leave at the gun range. Somebody will enjoy firing the ammo at paper targets."

"I owe you one."

"You've saved my butt several times. Once with a chainsaw, if memory serves." Max waved dismissively with the Five-Seven. "It all balances out."

TWENTY

WHEN SLATER GOT TO his house, he climbed out of the Thunderbird as the garage door rolled down. His phone had buzzed a minute ago, and he checked it now. It was a text from Andy:

> We need to talk. Can you be at the central market in an hour?

Slater thumb-typed a reply:

> I just saw you. Do you have more info about Lance?

His response came a moment later:

> Just be there.

"Idiot," Slater muttered, and tucked his phone away.

He might need his water backpack tomorrow, he decided, and pulled it off the tool rack. It was intended for trail running, with a water bladder inside and a mouth valve so you could drink without stopping or pulling it off. He'd found it extremely useful the last time he was in the desert.

In the back of the garage, at the sink next to the laundry machines, he filled the reservoir, then opened his gear cabinet to retrieve his satellite modem. In a flat black case, it was totally unmarked, like so much of Svetlana's tech. There was no guarantee of a cell signal in the Mojave, but there was plenty of open sky for this thing to connect. He tucked the battery in the pocket above the water bladder, then put the modem in the top pouch and connected the power cable.

There was something else he should do to prep for the trip, he realized. Hustling up the stairs, he pulled open his laptop and sat with it at the dining table. Pike said he should get a desk, as he had room for it in this big empty space, but he didn't need it— he had a desk already, at his office. The last thing he needed in his life was multiple freaking offices.

In an email, he copied the list of the homesteads he was going to visit tomorrow, each with latitude-longitude coordinates, and arranged them in the order he planned to hit them, starting with the Goff place. He set the message to send to Max late tomorrow night, just in case he didn't make it back.

Trotting down to his garage again, he found Svetlana's glasses, sitting on his workbench, still in the paper grocery bag. It was really lucky that he hadn't left them in his car. They were so obviously not regular glasses—the feds would have had a lot more questions for him last night.

Slater climbed in the Thunderbird and drove downtown, to the central market. A block up from it, he found an open meter and pulled in. Before he got out of the car, he found the power switch on the glasses, and slid it on with a fingernail, then pulled them on. They felt heavy but they didn't distort his vision. He wasn't doing anything shady tonight, but why let someone else's software create a list of his movements just from recording his face?

Walking into the market, he scanned the tables on this side, then walked through the crowded array of eateries and shops to the Broadway side. Andy and Kyle were here, sitting at a little table. It probably shouldn't irk him that they were together on the same side, all intimate and personal, but it did.

As he stepped up, Slater gestured to a tray with empty food containers and balled-up napkins on it. "I guess we're not having dinner together. Why do I have to meet you here, and not at your loft?"

"Because we'd wind up in bed," Andy said.

He dropped into the chair across from them. "What's wrong with that? Not so long ago I was the salsa in your white-bread sandwich."

"What's with the glasses?" Kyle said. "Is your monkey pox causing cognitive impairment?"

"It's called avant-garde style, sweetheart. I'm sure it'll trickle up to Beverly and Dana Point once some hipster-trash appropriates it for you. Wait a few months and lo, all the fashion victims floating around Newport Beach will be wearing these."

Kyle scowled. "I'm not from Orange County, you dick. And there's a difference between being avant-garde and just being a weirdo."

"We agreed we were … going to stay calm, remember?" Andy said.

"About what?" Slater demanded.

Andy took a deep breath, and his rhythmic muscle movements intensified. "We're getting married."

"Whoa." Slater sat back. "That's insane. How well do you actually know this guy? Have you even run a background check? I mean, does he steal? Is he after your money?"

"That's not your business," Kyle said. "The point is, no more sex with Andy."

"Or with you? I've been balls deep in you, Kyle, at more than one three-way. I didn't hear any complaints then. You were begging for all this." Slater gestured up and down his own torso, and mimicked Kyle: "Fuck you, you basic thug.'"

Kyle turned red and folded his arms.

"There's no need to be crass," Andy said. "This isn't about … you. It's about us. We're going exclusive."

"Kyle decided that?" Slater demanded.

"We both decided."

"So I'm just banned from your life?"

"Of course not. I just don't trust … myself. You're banned from my loft."

Slater scoffed.

"You have to admit you're a sex maniac," Kyle said. "You can come over if I'm there, or if you produce a written plan that we deem viable to keep your paws off him."

"You make me sound like a molester. It takes two to tango, Kyle."

"It's just for a while," Andy said. "Until we get … established."

"I couldn't do my job without you," Slater said. "I'd go broke."

"This doesn't change our … working relationship."

He glared at them and waved an arm. "A McMansion in Laguna, is that the plan? Matching Boston terriers, a Lexus and a Bimmer, marble countertops for an eight-hundred-dollar blender that nobody ever uses?"

Kyle flashed a palm. "I'm sure you're having feelings—"

"Shut up," Slater snapped. "Just shut the fuck up." He jabbed a finger at Andy. "And fuck you."

Rising, he strode away, and before he got to the street, paused to take a breath. He had to be rational right now, he knew that. He couldn't afford to burn this bridge.

"Fuck," he shouted.

The market was crowded, as it always was, and heads turned in his direction. A straight couple walking past him gave him a wary side-eye, and he saw a security guard in the distance turn toward him, his brow furrowing. Slater closed his eyes for a second and channeled all the shrinks he'd talked to through his youth. Striding back toward the tables, he found Andy and Kyle still sitting there.

Kyle looked up and saw him approaching. His eyes grew wide. "This is a public place, man." He gestured around the hall. "So many witnesses."

"I'm not going to punch you, you dipshit." He stood with his hands on his hips. "Mazel tov on making this decision. I respect the fact that you're being tits-out about what you want. Is there a ring?"

"We got matching ones," Andy said, and held out his hand. Kyle set his hand on the table too.

Slater sat and leaned over the table, grasping

Andy's hand to get a look. It was a simple gold band.

"Utilitarian," he said. "No bullshit. Typical Andy."

He could feel his throat closing up, like he couldn't breathe, and there was water in his eyes. He hoped they couldn't see that through the stupid stealthy glasses. Pulling back, he wiped his nose.

"I know you care about him," Slater said, eyeing Kyle. His own voice sounded weird, and hoarse.

Andy's face contorted. "Oh, Slater."

"You should invite Doris. She loves weddings. Invite me too, if you want. I promise I won't ruin it."

Rising, he walked away, back toward Hill Street and his car. It was embarrassing to be emotional like that, losing it, crying in public. The lump in his throat was actually painful, and there were more tears in his eyes. Why was this happening outside his conscious control? He really was an emotional wreck.

Outside on the street he dropped onto a bus bench, breathing hard, and pulled off the glasses to wipe his eyes. He deserved to be treated like trash, he knew that. He deserved to be battered by Andy. Slater had hurt him plenty. A sob shook his body, and caught in his throat.

"Are you OK? You look a little rattled."

He looked up to find a woman in a loud shift dress, form-fitting and in a psychedelic paisley print, her brow furrowed. She had dark Latin hair, and from the exaggerated makeup and the Adam's apple, she had to be a drag queen. There was a fun bar up the block with a dance floor, he knew. She must be headed there.

Slater took a breath. "I just got dumped." He wiped his eyes and snorted.

"Oh, sweetheart." She sat beside him, perched on the edge of the bench, her knees twisted toward him. "Women can be so cruel."

"She's a man. Actually a couple of them." He waved a hand. "It's a whole thing."

"It does get better," she said. "Eventually you have to get on your feet, and square your shoulders, and hold your head high."

"You're very compassionate."

"I know what it's like when a man puts you through the spin cycle. Plus it breaks my heart to see a pretty boy cry."

Slater chuckled and wiped his nose. "I don't get called that very often. Are you performing tonight, or just out on the town?"

"I'm with some friends. I'd say we're on a pub crawl, but that sounds a little trashy. You can join us if you'd like. Bathtub gin isn't a long-term solution, but it's one way to forget."

"I can't. But have fun." He rose with her. "Shoulders square, head high?"

She smiled. "That's it."

Once he was back at his house he trudged up to the kitchen, and pulled the fifth of bourbon out of the pantry cupboard, and poured a double. It felt like he'd just been cut off at the knees—he needed this. Taking a slug, he coughed at the fumes, and relished the fire, willing it to burn through him, burn the pain out.

Kyle would be good for Andy, he knew that. He had resources and he cared about the guy. He'd be loyal and supportive and connected. All the things Slater could never be.

Tumbler in hand, he went over to the sofa and

stretched out, then called Pike.

"Hey, forty-niner," Pike said when he answered. "What's up?"

"I just wanted to hear your voice."

"I get it. I miss you too. You sound tired."

They talked for a while, but not for too long. Slater just needed to connect. This guy was becoming the source of his stability, his roots, the thing that kept him upright. The monsoon rain on his dormant desert seeds. The person he wanted to be a better man for.

TWENTY-ONE

⧉⧉⧉⧉⧉⧉⧉⧉⧉⧉⧉

WAKING EARLY, AND TIMING his departure to miss the morning school traffic, Slater grabbed his water backpack and got on the freeway.

It was a long schlep east, with each microclimate getting warmer and drier as he crossed the intervening mountain ranges. He stopped for gas before he got too far out. Eventually, when the highway dropped into the Coachella Valley, it was full-on desert. As he turned north, the road gained several thousand feet in elevation as he rolled into the Mojave, and the look of the landscape changed. The back road to Barstow led him through a forest of Joshua trees, and when he got close to Landers, they thinned out as the land got flatter and more open.

The homesteads were far apart—this was definitely a place to go if you wanted privacy. His navigation app led him through a couple of turns onto narrow paved roads, then onto a dirt road, and a final turn onto a rough dirt double-track that led to the Goff place.

A gate across the road marked the property boundary. Slater pulled up to it and leaned toward the windshield to look it over. From the gateposts a barbed-wire fence stretched away in both directions across the desert. Its few strands wouldn't stop the wildlife or a determined pedestrian, but it would keep vehicles out. The gate was locked with a length of heavy chain and a padlock, and the sign on it read NO TRESPASSING—ARMED RESPONSE. A camera was mounted on one of the gateposts, and another one perched higher up, out of reach on a pole. That was an intriguing sign—either there was something valuable here, or somebody had something to hide. Whichever it was, they likely already knew he was here.

Pulling his phone out of its dash mount, he looked at the overhead satellite view of the property. The building site was on the opposite side, not visible from here, obscured by a gentle rise in the landscape. It looked to be maybe half a mile away, and the image showed that the double-track beyond the gate continued to it, leading across the dusty desert.

Shifting into reverse, Slater backed up and parked the Thunderbird a dozen yards back from the fence, tight to the side of the road, and climbed out. It was easy enough to scale the gate, as it was made of welded-together lengths of smooth steel pipe, meant to marshal livestock, with no razor wire or spikes to dissuade humans.

At the top he swung his leg over, then the other, and dropped onto the gritty pinky-tan ground on the inside. As he walked he sipped from his water backpack. It tasted a little plasticky but it was satisfying in the dry desert air.

When the building site came into view, it all looked smaller than it had from the satellite images. The trio of structures were more like minimalist shacks. One of them had its double doors propped open, and as he got closer, inside he could see a time-worn workbench, an ancient blackened vise, and an array of hand tools hanging on the wall. Next to the shack was a haphazard pile of lumber, and farther away was a neat stack of old tires. Beyond it he caught a glimpse of the solar array, the dark glassy panels angled toward the sun in the southern sky.

A dozen vehicles were parked around the structures. One was compressed into a buckled mess from a crash, and near the workshop an old Impala with no tires sat up on blocks. An SUV looked like it might be operable, as did the classic Crown Vic, and the pickup, and maybe the minivan.

As he got closer to the structures he called out "Hello" and clapped his hands a few times. He wasn't sure what the etiquette was in the high desert, but announcing his presence might make it less likely that he'd get shot at.

Near one of the shacks was a tuft of low cacti with a ring of rocks around it. Two wooden stakes were planted on the driveway side, their tops spray-painted fluorescent orange. He paused to look it over.

The door of the largest structure swung open, and a man stepped out. Dressed in a baggy work shirt and jeans, he was thin and sinewy, his white hair pulled back in a tail, white stubble on his face. Slater had half expected him to be carrying a firearm, but his hands were empty.

"I want to say this is a plains pricklypear," Slater said, gesturing to the cacti.

"You'd be right."

"I didn't think the varieties with the long spines grew this far south."

"They don't," he said, and put his hands on his hips. "That there is an erratic. That's why I tried to protect it."

"Good idea."

"You're trespassing. I know you climbed over a locked gate."

"And your name isn't really Goff. I can see the family resemblance. Harold has your eyes."

His eyebrows shot up, but he quickly masked his reaction, and hesitated before he spoke. "How did you find me?"

Lance was actually calm, Slater decided. He'd expected screaming and a brandished shotgun, but he wasn't there yet.

"It was a lot of freaking work."

"I hope so. I worked hard to disappear. Clearly not hard enough. How do you know Harold?"

"There was a custody dispute," Slater said. "His ex hired me to dig up dirt on him."

"Mary-Alice is a gorgon."

"I know that now. From what I saw Harold is actually a really good father."

"I'm glad to hear that."

"Harold said you did a mitzvah for his kid. Helped him set up a college fund."

"You're Jewish?" Lance said.

"Through my mother. I've been told by her relatives that my role in the family is to serve as a cautionary example for the youngsters."

He laughed. "Some of the early gangsters were Jewish. Like that guy who built Vegas."

"I'm not a gangster," he said.

"Are you sure about that? I saw you roll up in that '78 T-Bird."

Slater looked around the yard. "I can see you know cars. You've got enough of them."

"Is that not what you expected?"

"To hear some people tell it, I thought I might find you in a hut surrounded by severed heads on stakes."

Lance chuckled. "I don't know who you are, but I know some things."

"The name is Slater."

"I don't care," he said, raising his voice. "I have some tech out by the gate. With that vehicle, I know you're not government. I also know you're not armed."

"You have a metal detector out there?"

"Something like that. I'm thinking your phone isn't working, correct? There's no cell signal. The military base starts right over there." He gestured into the distance. "This whole area is a radio dead zone."

Slater spread his palms. "I'm not feeling the need to make any calls right now."

"Well, I have connectivity, and I'm going to make a call." He put his hands on his hips. "It'll set in motion a process that will take me far from here. I'll be long gone before you even get back into cell coverage to tell anybody."

"You have an evacuation service? I've heard of those. That takes serious resources."

"I have serious resources," Lance said. "Once I summon them, they'll show up, and I'll be gone. There won't be anything left here."

Except all the junked cars, Slater thought. Those weren't going anywhere. "Do they come by helicopter? That's extremely cool. I'm tempted to say go for it, just so I can watch."

He frowned. "It's not really your decision."

"I know that," Slater said. "Before you make the call, maybe we can just talk for a minute. Talk is cheap, right?"

"Is there anyone coming behind you?"

"If I tell you I'm alone, I'm afraid you'll try to croak me."

"I need to know whether you're stalling for time."

Slater groaned. It felt risky to be honest with the guy. But if Lance was going to plug him, he likely would have tried it already.

"No one else is coming."

"Not even Maximillian Conroy?" Lance said.

"Whoa." He frowned. "Where did that come from?"

"In the time it took you to walk over from the gate, I did a records search on your license plate. That gave me your name, and that led to a whole bunch of connections."

A license-plate frame with Svetlana's camera-jamming tech, Slater thought. That's what he needed next. He was totally going to mention it to her.

"So you already know who I am," Slater said. "Max isn't with me on this job. He's in LA this weekend peeping under window shades."

He nodded. "Do you drink coffee?"

"I'm not going to lie to you, Lance. I like my java." He threw up his hands. "Hit me."

Lance grinned and stepped back into the shack, and Slater followed him inside. It was a boxy space with a couple of windows, a bed and an easy chair, and a desk topped with a pair of wide computer screens. Along one wall were shelves loaded with books and boxes and a row of booze bottles, and high on another was the interior unit of a mini-split heat pump. Overhead the joists holding up the flat roof were exposed, and through the doorway at the back he could see a bathroom sink. In a corner sat a telescope on a tripod. Teresa had mentioned that—Lance was a stargazer.

"This is a homesteader cabin," Lance said, and stepped over to the workbench at the side of the room. It had a bar fridge under it and a hot plate on top with an espresso pot sitting on it. "The rule was they had to be at least ten by twelve, but whoever built this one went deluxe. It's about twenty by twelve."

"How old is it?"

"Early 1950s, maybe. The homesteading out here was finished by the seventies. The bathroom was an add-on sometime later." Lance poured from the espresso pot into a mug, then another, and handed one to Slater. "I just made it. It should still be warm."

Lance sat in the chair at his desk, a comfortable gaming model like Andy's, and motioned for Slater to take the easy chair. Slinging off his backpack, he set it on the floor as he sat down. He waited for Lance to drink first, then sipped at the mug. It was barely lukewarm but strong and nutty.

"That's good joe," Slater said.

"I know you're a mercenary, and I know why you're here," Lance said. "Wilma put a bounty on my head."

"It started out that way." He sat back and cradled the mug in his hands. "But I'm starting to question things. I talked to some of your old employees, and to Harold. The only person who says you're worth dropping a dime on is Wilma. And then Desiree tried to put the frame on me to get rid of one of their investors, and Wilma came after me with a goon who pulled a gun on me."

"She actually has a bodyguard?" Lance scoffed. "Which investor did they try to take down?"

"A guy named Boryan."

"The Serbian? He's not the kind of guy you mess with."

"I've met him," Slater said. "I'd say that's a valid assessment. It was nervy to go after him that way. And Wilma showing up with a gunslinger seemed downright desperate."

"I'm sure she is desperate. I keep tabs on her company. Despite what she tells people, it looks to me like she's on the brink of insolvency. I'm sure she's heavily in debt to people like Boryan. You can only limp along with the broken shell of a product for so long."

"It used to be your company too." Slater raised his eyebrows. "She says you ripped her off. Ripped off your investors."

"That's a lie," he snapped.

"I only know what Wilma told me."

"I didn't rip anyone off. I was very public about what was happening back then. Why does no one remember my side of it? I published an article warning people to cash out—weeks before I did that myself."

"Nobody told me that."

"I warned people, Slater," he said intently. "I warned Wilma. I told them the roof was about to fall in. That article was widely available in cryptospace. Nobody believed me. One guy actually said to my face, 'You poor old man. You've had your day. You're just out of touch with reality now.' That's when I decided I wasn't going to wait around for the collapse. I cleared out."

"If you warned her about what was coming, why is Wilma so pissed at you?"

"Because I was right. She said I was being alarmist, that I was foolish to cash out. At worst it'll be a correction, she said. Wilma knows damn well I spent months converting all my crypto holdings to real money before the crash, and now she wants a cut of it. As if she has any right to it. She still has her half." He scoffed. "What she had left after the crash was worth a fraction of a penny on the dollar. But that was her choice."

"So she could have done the same thing," Slater said, "but she chose not to? I guess it is a pretty big comedown for her. She's running a small business now, not a world-changing billion-dollar enterprise."

"More than that, she's desperate because the end is near. Messing with the Serbian is just plain suicidal." Lance leaned toward him and gestured with his cup. "If you're thinking of collecting that price Wilma put on my head, you're a chump. I know for a fact that her company doesn't have that much real money on hand. Almost everyone got laid off already. Even the lawyer. Your legal people are the last ones you should get rid of. She'll stiff you, brother, and I know how she'll do it—she'll give you a bunch of worthless coin at a speculative inflated value. When you tried to sell it, you might clear a few hundred dollars."

Slater looked away. "I've had dealings with her. I know you're right."

"Is that the only reason you came looking for me?" he said. "Wilma's vaporware reward?"

"I think part of it was the mystery. All the different versions of you that I heard. I got intrigued."

"What versions?"

"Well, Brandon Fox thinks you're dangerous," Slater said. "He said you're tangled up with the Russians."

"Who's Brandon Fox?"

"He used to be Miguel. From Wilma's TV series."

"That idiot." Lance scoffed. "Do you consider him a reliable source? He once told me the government was putting tracking devices in tubes of lip balm. 'Not other products?' I asked him. 'Not eyewash or toothpaste or aspirin bottles?' 'No,' he said, 'it's just lip balm. Because everyone carries one of those all the time. Nobody walks around with toothpaste in their pocket.'"

Slater laughed. "That does sound like Brandon. And that TV series. It kind of creeps me out."

"Everything about it was bizarre. Did Wilma do the voice for you?"

"Twice."

"She loves to do the voice." Lance set his cup

aside. "So there's no other reason you're here? I'm not just avoiding Wilma. Uncle Sam wants to talk to me too."

"The key word there is *talk*. The feds didn't put a price on your head. They don't want to bust you. And it's only the IRS—nobody but them gives a shit about your tax problems."

Lance smiled. "You're no dummy. You did your homework."

"I did, but I didn't have the whole story."

"Are you saying I don't have to deploy my ejector seat?"

"To be honest, Lance, you seem kind of boring. Not dangerous. And that million clams is starting to look pretty illusory." Slater drained his mug. "Activating your escape plan seems like a waste of time and resources. Don't upend your life because of me."

"You say that now. How do I know you won't drive back to LA and rat me out anyway?"

"If I do, you'll see them coming. You can engage your escape plan then."

"Not if they send a SWAT team or a helicopter gunship."

"They don't do that for tax scofflaws," Slater said, "and you know Wilma doesn't have that kind of resources."

Lance sat back, and his expression shifted.

"Good," he muttered, and then met his eye. "I feel sorry for you. No matter what you do, you're not going to get paid."

TWENTY-TWO

<hr>

"I HATE THAT I'M NOT going to get paid," Slater said. "It's absolutely infuriating. But that's not your fault. It's been in the back of my mind since they attempted the frame job. The way it went down implied that Wilma didn't really have the dough. I should have known then that it was too good to be true." Slater shrugged. "Maybe I can try to be content just to get out of town for the day. Enjoy the desert scenery, you know? It's a beautiful drive. Fresh air. I got to see a plains pricklypear today. How cool is that?"

"Extremely cool."

"It'll help me work it out of my system. The heady delusion of the big payday."

"I like this." Lance waved a hand. "Being able to talk to people. I find that if I can talk face-to-face, I can usually change their minds."

Slater frowned. "I'm pretty sure I changed my own mind. What I saw in Wilma's office, and Desiree's ham-fisted setup, and the gunslinging—it all fits with what you said, that she's broke, and in hock up to her neck. I needed to piece together all the little fragments of truth in everyone's twisted version of events. She lied to my face, but I don't think you have."

Lance nodded. "I don't really need to."

He eyed him for a moment. "You're not who I thought you were."

"I'm glad you see that." He chuckled. "Severed heads on stakes. The only severed heads I see are unfortunate jackrabbits, between the coyote's dinner and the turkey vulture's lunch."

"It's odd, the thing about disappearing," Slater said. "When there's no information about it, no facts, the void gets filled in anyway. Everyone made up their own version of what happened to you. You're taking the dirt nap in the Angeles National Forest, or you're working with the Russians in St. Petersburg, or you're drinking mai tais on a beach."

"I'm sure it's confounding. The only way to leave this world is to die, but I was taken to the spirit world without the agency of death."

Slater's eyes narrowed. "It doesn't look like you're in the spirit world to me."

"People think I am. Buried in a shallow grave or sitting on a generic beach is almost the same thing. I'm outside their reality and forever unreachable."

"Someone told me you were a deep thinker," Slater said. "I can't imagine you get a lot of opportunities for Socratic dialogue. How many visitors do you get out here?"

"It does get lonely sometimes. But then I drive to the supermarket and the hardware store and I interact with some other humans. That balances me out for a while."

"Opportunities for sex must be pretty thin on the ground."

Lance laughed. "That's an accurate characterization."

"Do you want me to smoke you before I go? I'm already here."

His eyebrows shot up. "Are you kidding me?"

"I don't joke around about the important stuff, son."

"You condescending ass." He scoffed. "I'm old enough to be your father."

"It can't get sticky, though. I'm in a relationship with this guy. I think I'm allowed to have sexual experiences but not romantic experiences."

"You think? You haven't clarified that with him?"

Slater threw up his hands. "Relationships and romance, man. It's like watching an Italian movie without the subtitles. I can hear the words, and I think I know what's going on, but big chunks of it are still a mystery."

"Matters of the heart are definitely a central conundrum of the human condition."

Setting his cup on the adjacent bookshelf, Slater eyed him and squeezed his crotch. "So are we going to do this?"

"My god," Lance said. "Where did you come from?"

"Los Angeles. I thought we'd established that already."

"I haven't bathed in a while."

He sat up and started to untie his boots. "I'm not

afraid of a little man-stank. It's to be expected from a desert rat."

Lance stood, and Slater rose to face him, and unbuckled his own belt, then put his hands on his hips, and raised his eyebrows, a tacit challenge. Reaching for his fly, Lance tentatively unbuttoned Slater's jeans. Slater stepped close, and grabbed his belt, then roughly unzipped his pants and shoved them down. Lance was breathing hard, his eyes bright.

Pushing him down onto the bed, Slater watched as he unbuttoned his shirt, then climbed on beside him. It was a good mattress. Even though he was living in the sticks, Lance had his comforts—a firm bed, air-conditioning, lots of booze. Shifting beside him, Slater grabbed his flaccid cock and squeezed.

"I'm a little nervous," Lance said. "It's been a long time."

"You don't have to perform for me. Just relax." He kissed his neck, and ran a hand over his chest, eliciting a sigh.

"I want to see your body," Lance said.

He sat up and pulled off his shirt, and moved to the side of the bed to ditch his jeans. Lance caressed his pecs, and his leg, and then his belly.

"You're hard," Lance said, and took hold of his cock.

Pressing into his hand, Slater leaned closer, folding a leg over his, and ground his cock into his thigh, then took a moment to nibble his stubbly jaw and explore his mouth with his tongue.

Lance pulled back. "I don't think I'll be able to, you know, go all the way."

"There's no rules. We can do whatever you want."

Slater ran his hand across his chest. "You manage to stay in shape out here."

"I know I look like I just got out of a concentration camp. But thank you for lying to me. Can I smoke you?"

"Who's ever going to say no to that?"

He shifted down, and took him into his mouth, working him intently. Watching him in action, Slater built up to it, his body vibrating, and strained into him as he came. Red-faced and panting, Lance moved up beside him.

"That was amazing."

Slater met his warm mouth, and grabbed his cock, still soft, and gently stroked it.

"I'm not sure if I'll be able to accomplish anything," Lance said.

He'd been with guys like this before, full of insecurity, when it had been too long between hookups. It just took time. Slater spent a minute caressing his torso, and his legs, intermittently squeezing his cock. He mouthed his neck, and his jaw, and his nipples, and briefly pulled him into a tight embrace. Eventually Lance got hard, and he pulled him close, kissing his neck and his ear, and stroked him hard and fast. When Lance climaxed, his whole body shuddered.

Once Lance had started to relax again, Slater rolled onto his back and folded his arm over his eyes, listening to him catch his breath.

"You're a lot of man, Slater."

Drifting toward sleep, he mumbled an acknowledgment.

"Do you want to hang around for a while? We can do that about twice a day."

He lifted his arm. "I probably shouldn't have done it at all. I need to keep my dick out of my cases."

Lance chuckled and got up, stepping into the bathroom. He didn't close the door, and Slater heard water running.

"How much gravy did you clear when you left?" Slater called to him. "Online sources were vague."

"I can tell you about all that," Lance said, and stepped back into the room, and tossed him a hand towel. "But first maybe you can help me with a little work."

"Around here?" He frowned. "No way. Hire a damn day laborer."

Lance stepped into his jeans and zipped up his fly. "It's more complicated than that. I suspect you know what it's like to get your hands dirty."

Sitting up, Slater shifted to the side of the bed and grabbed his shirt. "I do. Literally and metaphorically."

"Your job is as a mercenary, right? What other countries have you worked in?"

"I'm an insurance investigator. I rarely leave LA County. I look at lots and lots and lots of fraud. Fake work injuries, missing jewelry that's not really missing, people stealing from cargo shipments."

Buttoning his shirt, Lance frowned. "Well, that's prosaic. I assumed it was just a cover story. Scanning the stuff about you online, I thought maybe you were some kind of international operative. You were able to track me down, so I figured you were hobnobbing with drug lords and arms dealers, chartering airplanes with fake passports, working with an office building full of crack researchers."

"I have an office, and it's in a building. But you

already knew that if you found Max. I have one very good researcher."

"How did he find me?"

"He didn't. He just gave me a general location. I looked at a lot of homesteads out here."

"How did he get my general location?"

"I don't know the details," Slater said, "but he's good at data analysis. Crunching numbers and connecting the dots. Apparently you've been trolling Wilma online."

"That, I have." He watched Slater for a moment. "I guess there's a price to pay for everything."

Slater stood up and buttoned his fly. "What is it you want me to help you with?"

Dropping into his desk chair, Lance met his gaze. "I need to acquire an engine for a 1970 Impala. It's near here. The current steward of that item refuses to sell it to me."

"I saw the Impala in your yard. It needs rims and tires."

"It also needs an engine."

"And you want to steal it?"

"Can such an important cultural artifact belong to any one individual? Who owns the *Mona Lisa*, or Yosemite Valley?"

"That would be the French people," Slater said, "and the American people, respectively."

"That engine is an American classic, and I'm one of the American people. It belongs to the world." Lance scowled. "It shouldn't be rusting out in that idiot's junkyard. Who says he gets sole control of it?"

Slater waved impatiently. "The police, the courts, the constitution."

"He won't even miss it."

"Why would you jeopardize all this?" He gestured to the room. "You worked so hard to disappear."

"There's no risk. We're not going to get caught."

"If you have enough dough to have an evacuation service, why not just buy a different engine? It's the 350 or the 396, right? They made those for years and years. There must be thousands of them."

"It's the 396. This one is special. Plus this guy was rude to me."

Slater put his hands on his hips. "Now it sounds like a personal beef."

"I know you value beautiful cars. You're driving one."

"How about this? I'll help you on the condition that you're telling me the truth about that article. The one you said you wrote that sounded the alarm about the crypto crash."

"A minute ago you said you'd decided I wasn't lying to you. Now you're saying you don't believe me."

"All day long I slosh around in the cesspool," Slater said. "Everybody lies to me all the time. It's the default setting. Just give me a couple minutes to convince myself that you're not playing me."

"Fine." Lance gestured broadly. "Whatever you need."

He picked up his backpack. "I'm going to step outside. My modem needs a view of the sky."

"Are you kidding me?" he demanded. "All this time you've had connectivity?"

"Technically I haven't. I never switched it on."

"Mother fucker. Show me the modem."

Suppressing a grin, Slater zipped open the

backpack's top pouch, and handed him the bag. Lance pulled out the device and turned it over in his hand.

"It's wired into a battery pack?"

"That's right."

"It's so small," he said. "This is next-gen. No way is this a consumer product."

"I needed it for when I was out in Nevada. There's not a lot of cell towers in the depths of the Great Basin."

"I've been out of the loop for too long. Who built it?"

"I work with a Russian electronics vendor," Slater said.

"I knew it. You are a damn mercenary."

He chuckled. "I'm an insurance investigator."

"It's a good cover."

"It's the truth."

"You don't have to go outside," Lance said, handing him the bag back. "You can use my Wi-Fi. Give me your phone."

Slater dug it out, and unlocked it, and handed it over, then watched as Lance tapped at it for a moment.

"You're connected," he said, and gave it back.

"So what am I looking for?"

"Search for my name and Crypto Buzz Daily. It's a website."

Slater sat in the easy chair and thumb-typed the words, only vaguely aware that Lance had scooted his chair over to his desk and started interacting with his computer.

Slater read aloud the title of the first item that came up: "The Impending Fall of Crypto."

"That's it," Lance said, swiveling toward him. "Check the date on the piece. That was nine weeks before I cleared out."

"Give me a minute."

Scrolling down the article, he found the familiar corporate headshot of Lance. Compared to his current persona, he looked so much younger, clean-shaven, with darker hair and a conservative haircut. The text contained a lot of technical jargon, but he slogged through it anyway. Finally he read aloud a direct quotation from Lance.

"'I can't see current coin values as sustainable. We're due for a massive correction across crypto-space. A lot of people are going to get spanked.'"

Lance swiveled to meet his gaze. "What did I tell you?"

"You knew the crash was coming."

"If you read the comments, you'll see all the push-back. No one believed me. They wanted my head on a pike."

"I can't understand why they didn't give you more credibility," Slater said. "You were a big name in crypto then."

"Nobody likes a pessimist, and no one wanted to hear bad news. Things were rolling along so well. Why pump the brakes?"

"That does sound like human nature."

"They said I was Chicken Little, but I'm god-damn Cassandra."

Slater tucked his phone away. "Given the gift of prophecy by Apollo but destined never to be believed."

"I can't believe you know who she is."

"The boyfriend and I have been reading Ovid."

"You are such a weirdo."

"I hear that a lot. The other classical analogy for you is Prometheus. You brought the world a shiny billion-dollar product, and now you're chained to a rock." Slater waved at the room.

"I don't mind this rock. It's a perfect place for stargazing." He gestured to the telescope standing in the corner. "The view of the Andromeda Galaxy through that baby would make your jaw drop."

"I believe you."

He cocked his head. "So if I'm Prometheus, does that make you Heracles?"

"I'm not here to save you, Lance. You have to do that yourself. Or call your evacuation service. But I will help you get that 396."

TWENTY-THREE

L ANCE CLAPPED HIS HANDS and hissed, "Yes."

Slater had to grin. "I'm sure you've formulated a plan."

"It's very simple. You'll go into this guy's yard and distract him. He's an idiot by the name of Vogel. Then I'll pull in and acquire the block."

"You can do that on your own?"

"Did you see my pickup? It has a crane mounted in the bed. I've got chains and everything. How are you at acting?"

"I know how to lie. That's basically the same thing." Slater waved a hand. "I need to know what kind of place this is. Does Vogel have cameras, employees, alarms?"

"None of that. He's a cranky old desert rat with acres and acres of wrecked cars. The hoarder type—there's so many cars that he doesn't even know what he's got. I need ten minutes to sneak in behind you and load up the engine."

"Won't it take longer than that to unbolt it from the vehicle it's in? Are you planning to use a cutting torch? That might be loud."

"No need for that. I've seen it. I've touched it with these hands." Lance held up his palms. "It's already out of the original vehicle and sitting on railroad ties."

"Show me an overhead view of his place."

Lance swiveled back toward his desk and grabbed his keyboard, then pulled up an image and pointed to the screen. "This is the front gate. The engine is right around here."

"That's near the road in. Convenient."

Dropping to one knee beside his chair, Slater grabbed the mouse and panned across the image. This photo wasn't the publicly available stuff—Lance had shelled out for the high-resolution view, the same way he had.

"It looks like the land gradually drops toward the south," Slater said. "If I can shift the guy's attention to that part of his property, you could work without being seen or heard. But how do I get him over to the far side of his land?"

They spent some time discussing strategy, and finally settled on a plan, and talked through the details. Lance had clearly been plotting this for a while, and had a lot of the minutia worked out. He got up and stepped around behind the bed and started to dig through his overstuffed clothes rack. Eventually he pulled out a tan-colored jacket with an oval patch on the left breast that was embroidered with the name BUTCH. He tossed it to Slater, and he shrugged it on.

"It fits you," Lance said.

He shoved his hands in the pockets. It was

lightweight, and actually pretty comfortable. "I wish I had a business card to give him."

"Let's print one out. We just need cardstock."

Standing in front of his shelves, Lance pulled books out, one after another, and briefly flipped open the covers. Finally he picked one, a dusty blue hardback, and set it on his desk. He dropped into his chair and used a utility knife to slice out a page, the heavy blank one just inside the back cover. Tossing the book aside, he turned to his computer, and spent a minute with a design program. Slater sat in the easy chair and watched from a distance as the card started to take shape on the screen. Lance typed a few lines, and adjusted the size, and then plugged in the image of a shield-shaped logo.

"Your fake office is in San Bernardino," Lance said, still focused on the screen. "People up here resent the fact that they're governed from so far away. From that tiny urban corner of the county."

"So Butch drove up from San Bernardino today."

He sat back and gestured to the screen. "How does that look?"

Slater rose and leaned in to study the image. "Butch Hernandez?"

"You have to admit you look like a Hernandez, more than you look like a Takahashi or a MacGowan."

"I can't argue with that."

Lance fed the heavy paper from the back of the book into his printer, and printed out the card, then used the utility blade and a ruler to trim it to the right size. He handed it to Slater.

"I'm thinking that's not a real phone number," he said, looking it over.

"The exchange is for a county office, but the number doesn't work."

Slater tucked the card in his pocket. "Vogel is a car guy, isn't he? I can't take my own wheels. The Thunderbird is too memorable. It got me into trouble when I was surveilling Harold—he remembered my ride and came over to punch me in the face."

Lance chuckled. "Harold always had a quick temper. You can take the minivan."

"That doesn't quite fit with the image of a county bureaucrat. Why not the Tahoe? That's suitably bland."

"He's seen me in that. It's my everyday ride."

"Is the Crown Vic running?" Slater said. "Governments bought lots of those when they were still making them."

"Almost. It needs a battery."

"So let's take the one out of the Tahoe."

When they went outside, the sun was noticeably higher in the sky. It felt warm for winter, but in the desert the days were usually warm, when it wasn't windy or raining.

The pickup did have a crane in the back, he saw. Mounted at the side of the bed, it was black and folded closed, making it look like a mast or a flagpole. But it was pro gear, with hydraulic lines running from the slender pistons, and a couple of control handles—Lance would have no trouble lifting a heavy big-block engine with it.

Lance stepped into the shed and grabbed a toolbox, and soon had the hood up on the Tahoe. Switching batteries wasn't a big job, and Slater helped him with it, holding the tools while Lance did the wrenching, and then carrying the heavy battery over to the Crown Vic.

Once they'd connected it, Slater got in behind the wheel and twisted the key. The engine started easily, and Lance shouted "Yeah," grinning like an idiot.

"Purring like a kitten," Slater called to him.

"It's the best car ever made."

He killed the engine and climbed out. "There's another problem." He pointed to the front end of the Crown Vic. "This has civilian tags. Do you think he'll notice?"

"Vogel is a dickwad, but he's sharp. He'll totally see that." Lance snapped his fingers. "I actually have a set of exempt plates."

Slater followed him over to the dramatically compacted wreck he'd noticed on the way in. It had been a white pickup, maybe, and it did have an intact exempt tag on the remnants of the back end. Whatever government agency it had belonged to had peeled off their logo, leaving its vague outline on the paint.

With a minute of screwdriver work, Lance pulled the plate, handing the rear one to Slater and then stepping around to the front. This one was in good shape, but the front one was a little mangled. Lance went into the workshop, and set it on the bench, then spent a minute pounding it with a rubber mallet. Eventually it looked flat and mostly presentable, and Slater helped him swap the tags onto the Crown Vic.

"I'd say we're ready," Slater said.

"The best time to catch Vogel will be in about forty minutes."

"You know his schedule?"

"It's all about averages and estimates," Lance said. "You know I'm a numbers guy. Come inside."

Slater followed him into the cabin, and Lance sat in his desk chair.

"Can you entertain yourself for a while?" Lance said. "I have some computer stuff to do."

"Are you going to trash-talk Wilma some more using one of your aliases?"

Lance frowned. "Clearly that's a suboptimal idea if it brought you here. I wish I knew how your researcher spotted me doing that."

"Something about anonymizing servers," Slater said, and gestured vaguely as he sat in the easy chair.

"I guess I knew that was risky. I'd like to talk to this person."

"I'll set it up with him if you're willing to give me a phone number. I know he'd be happy to explain it all."

"Excellent."

He swiveled to face his screen, and Slater pulled out his phone to look over the aerial view of the target junkyard again. There were so freaking many cars on Vogel's land, arranged in long uneven aisles. It didn't look like they were piled on top of each other, but even in a single layer there had to be hundreds of them. He went through the plan again in his head, and rehearsed his story, and repeated his alias and his bogus job title so that it would be fluid in his mind.

Eventually Lance rose, and grabbed a narrow-brimmed straw hat from a nail next to the door, and set it on his head. "I'm ready."

Slater tucked his phone away and followed him outside and over to the vehicles.

"Wait until I get it running," Lance said. "Just in case."

Climbing into the Crown Vic, Slater started it and looked to Lance. He heard the pickup's engine catch. It sounded smooth and well-tuned. Lance revved it, and let it settle, then flashed him a thumbs-up.

He nosed the car onto the double-track that led toward the road. Even on the dirt the Crown Vic rode smooth. He stopped in front of the gate and eyed the Thunderbird through the bars. Lance pulled up behind him, and hopped out, and unlocked it. After he'd pushed it open, Slater rolled his window down and drove through.

"I'll wait for your signal," Lance said as he strode past, headed back toward his pickup.

It was a few miles to the junkyard, on dirt roads, and then a paved road, and then back on the dirt. The gate to the place hung open. Slater nosed into the yard, and parked the Crown Vic, and climbed out.

Waiting for the guy to appear, as Lance assured him he would, Slater adjusted the jacket, and rolled his shoulders, and arched his back, as if he'd been in the car for a long time. As promised, the guy stepped out of a trailer parked near the driveway. Scowling and wearing grubby coveralls, he was a sunbaked white guy, with gray hair and deeply lined skin. He could be Lance's brother. As he stepped out he pulled a ball cap onto his head, but of more concern was the shotgun in his other hand, currently pointed at the dirt rather than at Slater.

"Mr. Vogel?" Slater called to him. "I'm not armed."

"What do you need?" he said, approaching the car.

"My name is Butch Hernandez. County health and safety." He held up the bogus business card.

Vogel stepped closer, and took it, and studied it. "You're from the city." He looked up. "You're working on Saturday?"

Why hadn't he or Lance even thought of that? No self-respecting civil servant would be on the job on the weekend.

"We work when there's trouble," Slater said. "Your neighbor down the wash says you've got a malfunctioning septic tank. It's leaking onto his property."

Vogel scowled. "That's bullshit."

"I walked the adjoining land," Slater said. "The wash drops pretty rapidly from your property line. There's definitely something happening there."

"My septic is nowhere near there, Butch."

"Could it be something else? A leak from a vehicle? RVs have onboard septic."

"I don't have anything like that by the wash."

"I'm afraid I'll have to take a look at that area," Slater said. "You can come with me."

"Damn right I'm coming with you. You're not going to snoop around unsupervised. I've got millions of dollars' worth of auto parts here."

Slater flashed his palms. "Lead the way."

He turned and walked to the trailer and stepped inside for a moment. When he came out again he no longer had the shotgun. Pulling the door closed, he locked it with a key on a bulky key ring, attached to his belt on a spring-loaded cable, like a janitor or a night security guard.

Vogel stepped over to a golf cart, and climbed on, and started the motor. It was more than a golf cart,

Slater realized, as it had a gas engine and all-terrain tires. He waved for Slater to get on. As he walked over, Slater double-keyed the walkie-talkie in his jacket pocket. It was the signal to Lance that they were moving away from the gate.

The rough two-stroke engine rumbled as Vogel drove between the rows of vehicles. The junkers actually were stacked in some places, two and three high, all of them with a coating of pinky-tan Mojave dust.

"I can't believe the county put you in that Crown Vic," Vogel said, raising his voice over the engine noise. "It must be twenty years old."

"It could be," Slater said. "There's lots of hoopties in the motor pool. It runs all right, though. It climbed the Yucca Grade like it was idling at a stoplight."

Vogel chuckled. "It's such a great vehicle. I guess I should be happy you didn't show up in a shiny new Navigator, since it's my tax dollars."

In a minute they were at the fence line. On wheels it wasn't far—that was not optimal. If Vogel happened to hear Lance's truck or his thievery operation, he could make it back there in seconds.

Vogel parked the cart and stepped off, leaving the key in the ignition. In the brief moment that Vogel's back was turned, Slater grabbed the key as he climbed off, tucking it in his front pocket. He might need to delay things later.

"Is the fence at the property line?" Slater said, looking it over. Like Lance's perimeter fence, it was made of metal stakes and three strands of barbed wire.

"Right on it." Vogel stepped up to it and gestured down the wash. "Where exactly is the problem? Are they sure they were smelling sewage? A rodent midden has that same kind of smell. It could be kangaroo rats or ground squirrels."

"It's a little farther down. I don't see any evidence of a spill right here, but I need to walk the fence."

Vogel adjusted his cap and walked abreast, and Slater scrambled mentally to come up with questions for him. That way Vogel would be less likely to press him on the fictional complaint or his nonexistent work.

"How long have you been here?" Slater said.

"It's family land. I grew up on this place."

"Was it farmland?"

"My mom had some horses," Vogel said, "but I was more interested in cars."

"I can see that. You sell auto parts?"

"Sometimes."

They reached the corner of the property, where the fence turned a right angle and stretched back toward the gate. Slater put his hands on his hips and gazed out across the landscape.

"You can see there's nothing here," Vogel said, and waved impatiently.

"So where is your septic?"

"Right beside the house. Back where you parked the Crown Vic."

He hadn't noticed a house, which meant it was out of view behind the wrecks. Or maybe it was that trailer he'd locked the shotgun in.

"I guess we can go."

They walked back to the cart, and as Vogel climbed on, he muttered, "Damn it."

"Problem?"

"Where's the freaking key?"

It had been long enough, Slater decided, and stealthily dug it out of his pants. As Vogel leaned out to look on the ground, he reached for the floor in front of the seat and held it up.

"It must have fallen out," he said, and handed it to him.

They rode back to where the Crown Vic was parked, and Vogel killed the engine, and they climbed off. Slater wasn't sure exactly where the 396 had been, but there was no sign of Lance's pickup.

"So what happens now?" Vogel said.

"I check a box on a form. I didn't see any evidence of septic problems here." Slater shrugged. "It must be something else. Maybe a rodent midden, like you said."

"It's that Dave guy, isn't it," Vogel said. "He wears the snakeskin boots."

"It was a woman who called it in. Carmela something, or maybe it was Charlotte."

"I don't know her. Sounds like she's got a sensitive nose."

"Well, you've got nothing to worry about," Slater said, and waved as he climbed into the Crown Vic.

TWENTY-FOUR

N THE WAY BACK toward Lance's place, Slater kept an eye on the rearview, but Vogel had no reason to follow him, and nobody else was on these back roads. The gate was still open at Lance's, and he rolled past the Thunderbird, and stopped once he was inside. Climbing out, he pushed the gate closed and snapped the padlock on the chain.

As he pulled into the yard, he saw that the engine block was sitting in the bed of the pickup. It had the transmission attached, and looked old and grubby, but it was hard to tell what condition it was in.

Lance was standing next to the cab, beaming at him as he got out of the Crown Vic.

"You did it," he said. "Look at this baby. Big-block V-8, overhead valves, damn near four hundred horsepower."

"A true national treasure," Slater said.

"Come in and tell me what happened."

Inside the cabin Lance sat at his desk, and Slater

took the easy chair, and they talked through it. Lance had lots of questions about what had been said, and tangentially dissed Vogel, and then explained how he'd been able to quickly wrap chains around the engine and hoist it into his pickup.

"Do you think he'll put it together that the engine disappeared when I was there?" Slater said finally.

"He's got so much stuff," Lance said. "He might not notice it for months. He might not even remember it."

"Earlier today you told me he was sharp."

"Did you see all the vehicles in that yard? How could anyone keep track of it all?"

"I guess if he's going to complain," Slater said, "it'll be about Butch Hernandez from the city, not about you or me."

"Do you like bourbon?" Lance rose and grabbed a bottle from his bookshelf.

"I don't mind a taste." It fit with his booze rules—he was working, but it was just the one, and he was with someone.

Lance poured a finger into each of two drinking glasses, and handed one to Slater as he stood up, and they clinked them together.

"Damn," he said, once he'd taken a sip. "This is good stuff." Why did everybody have better booze than he did?

"Now I have a project for the rest of the winter," Lance said.

"Rebuild that 396."

"And restore the Impala."

Slater savored another mouthful. "You owe me a story."

"Fair enough." Lance chuckled and dropped into his desk chair, waving Slater back into the easy chair. "I was pretty sure the day of reckoning for crypto was coming, as you saw in that article, but I couldn't just cash out all my coin at once. That alone would have made its value tank. I had to spread it around. I bought other financial assets, even some other coin that was stable, and traded that for dollars and euros. The multiple formats and serial transactions made them less visible. Eventually I managed to convert almost everything to cash, and put it in a tax haven."

"South Dakota," Slater said, "or Luxembourg, or the Cayman Islands."

"One of those."

"How much?"

"A lot."

"Enough to have an extraction service ready on demand."

Lance nodded. "Exactly."

"I've never really known much about money." Slater sat back. "I've acquired it, in big amounts and small amounts, and stacked it up, and spent it. It wasn't that important to me. But then I went and bought a house. I owe the bank half a million on it. I can feel how much money that is, and what it means—I've thought about it, and I live in the middle of it. Would your assets be a hundred times that much? A thousand times?"

He pursed his lips for a moment. "Doing the math in my head, it would be several thousand times that much."

Slater laughed. "Right on. My mother would call you a *macher*. Why don't you go to Bermuda, and splash your dough around, and bag yourself a boyfriend? Live like a Mediterranean capo instead of a desert rat."

"I'm no capo. I actually don't mind being on my own."

"I guess that's what they meant by the pursuit of happiness. Whatever works for you." Slater drained his glass. "I should go."

As he rose and pulled on his backpack, Lance spoke.

"Just to be clear, if you send anyone after me, I'll know they're coming. Like I knew you were coming."

"I'm not going to do that. I know there's nothing in it for me, and I know you didn't do anything wrong. Wilma's the real crook." He waved a hand. "And don't take this personally, but I don't care what you do."

"Like you told the public prosecutor. 'I don't care whether you live or die,' you said."

Slater frowned. "How do you know that? It happened, like, a week ago."

"Everything said in open court is public record. There's a transcript. I did more reading on you while we were waiting to go rescue the 396."

"That feels a little nosy."

"You can understand my curiosity. You did manage to find me when I didn't want to be found. And the transcript did tell me more about who you are."

"You're not sure whether you should trust me."

"I like that you're disinterested," Lance said. "It's reassuring. Plus you did commit what the authorities would consider fraud to help me out with that engine. But are you any good at keeping secrets?"

"This Russian woman I know says, 'Two people can keep a secret if one of them is dead.' Personally I'd prefer you use your escape hatch rather than grease me."

"The reason I have an evacuation service is so that I don't have to do things like that." Lance got up. "I want to give you something. An incentive to keep my secrets."

He pulled a box down from above the books, one of a dozen lined up on a high shelf, and handed it to Slater. It was made of graying unfinished wood, and held together with rusty staples, with a bourbon logo burned into one side.

"Is this the stuff we were drinking?" Slater said. "That was mighty fine bourbon. Is it a fifth, or a whole handle? It's so damn heavy." He heaved the box in his hands. "Part of me thinks this might be an explosive device, and it'll go off when I climb over your gate, and turn me into a pink cloud." He raised his eyebrows. "Dead men tell no tales."

"Why would I do that?" Lance demanded. "It would summon the authorities right to my door. If I were building a bomb, I'd set it up to go off with air pressure. When you drove down into the Coachella Valley, on the rural part of the highway before you got to the city, so there'd be less chance of collateral damage."

His eyes narrowed. "That was awfully close to the top of your mind, Lance. Is this really just bourbon?"

"Open it if you want. I can get you a screwdriver. Or if you're really suspicious of it, just leave it here."

"It feels like that would be rude," Slater said. "Like I didn't trust you."

"I know you don't trust me. You just speculated that I might be about to assassinate you."

"I did help you commit a felony today. That implies you and I have a degree of mutual trust."

"But it's not unconditional," Lance said. "I get that."

"How about I open it when I get to my car? That way I can drive back to the city without worrying about it. If it blows up there, it'll summon the authorities right to your door."

"It's not going to blow up. Why would I give you a bomb? I have your plate number, and I know where you work. Like you said, I could easily send an assassin after you."

"Dude," Slater said intently.

Lance laughed. "I jest. You've seen enough of me to know that's not who I am. The box is a small thank-you for helping me out, and for keeping my secrets."

He studied his face for a moment. "I guess I believe you."

"Do you want a ride to the gate?"

"So you can watch me blow up?"

Lance frowned. "So you don't have to walk, you dick."

"The walk will be good for me. I've got a long drive ahead. Call me when you get that Impala running." Slater jutted his chin. "You and I'll drive out to Amboy and drink some more of the good stuff."

As he stepped outside, he paused to look over the pricklypear again. It looked healthy and content. Lance might have watered it once in a while but he wasn't spoiling it.

The bourbon box was bloody heavy, and it was an awkward size, too big to fit in his sleek little backpack. As he walked toward the gate he shifted it from one arm to the other, sometimes carrying it with both.

At the fence he shoved the box underneath, then climbed over the gate, and carried it to the Thunderbird. Opening the trunk, he found a jimmy, and set the box on the ground a few yards from the vehicle, and squatted next to it with his back to the car. Just in case. If it really was an IED, it would likely send him into the next world, but there was no need to mess up such a beautiful machine.

When he pried the top off the box, he had to focus for a second to parse what he was seeing. There was no bottle inside. At first it looked like books, packed in tightly with the edges of the pages facing up, but then he realized the box was stuffed with cash—neat bundles of bills wedged in sideways, bound with blue elastic bands. He pulled out a bundle and flipped through it. The bills weren't new, but they were all hundreds. Digging deeper he found more of the same underneath.

In his head he did a quick calculation. There were about thirty bundles here. If they were all C-notes, thirty racks meant about three hundred grand. He could almost pay off his house with this.

Slater had to laugh. He'd have to give some of it to Andy, of course, as he'd done a lot of the work. But still, this was almost as good as Wilma's spurious reward. From what Lance had told him, the guy could definitely afford such largesse.

Stepping back to the gate, Slater waved at the camera mounted there. "Lance—you're nuts. I would have kept your secrets for free. But thank you."

Once he'd packed the box in the trunk, he fired up the Thunderbird, and turned around, and drove slow on the bumpy dirt road. It was a few miles back to the pavement, and he was in for several hours behind the wheel, but he couldn't help but feel a little buzzed. He wasn't going to shanghai Lance and haul him back to the city, and Wilma wouldn't get her Wild West showdown with the guy. But the trip had paid off anyway.

———◆———

www.ingramcontent.com/pod-product-compliance
Lightning Source LLC
Chambersburg PA
CBHW010843190726
48286CB00012BA/2959